CW00506166

# THE DETECTIVE'S SECRETARY

by

Tara J. Stone

© 2020 by Tara J. Stone
Self-published
(tjstone0828@gmail.com)

All rights reserved.
No part of this publication may be reproduced, stored in a
retrieval system, stored in a database and/or published in any
form or by any means, electronic, mechanical, photocopying,
recording, or otherwise, without the prior written permission of
the publisher.

FADE IN:

INT. IRENE'S APARTMENT - BEDROOM - MORNING (1938)

IRENE GRANGER (20s) studies her reflection in a full-length mirror.

If it weren't for her frown, wire-rimmed glasses, and impeccably tasteful ladies' suit, Irene could be the next pin-up girl.

Behind her, papers and photos litter the floor, the bed, a chair, the top of the dresser. Newspaper and magazine clippings. Handwritten scraps. Official police reports and court records. Mugshots.

In Irene's hand is a .38 Colt Detective Special.

She stuffs the revolver into the back of her waistband and turns to the side to see how much it sticks out.

She grabs a tweed jacket that matches her skirt from the back of a chair and tugs it on, but the revolver makes it too tight to button.

She pulls once. Twice. Finally gets a button through a hole.

Turns to the side again. Awful.

                    IRENE
          Ugh. "Excuse me, miss, I think you
          have a pistol-shaped tumor growing
          on your back."

Disgusted, she unbuttons the jacket and tries the gun in the front of her waistband.

                    IRENE (CONT'D)
          Oh, brother.

She tries again to hide it with the jacket, but when she finally gets the front pulled together, a BUTTON POPS OFF and flies across the room.

With a sigh, she takes the pistol out and ponders her reflection again.

A beat.

She hitches up her skirt to her thigh and sticks the gun in her garter. When she lets the skirt back down, the bulge on her thigh is more than noticeable.

And then the GUN CLATTERS to the floor.

                    MARJORIE (O.S.)
         Everything okay in there?

Irene picks up the gun, frustration mounting.

                    IRENE
            (calling)
         Yeah, just swell!

Maybe inside her bra strap?

Nope, that's the worst idea yet.

INT. IRENE'S APARTMENT - KITCHEN - SAME

Irene's roommate, MARJORIE (20s), drinks a cup of coffee
and eats a piece of toast at the table. She still has her
hair pinned up in curlers and a bathrobe on.

Irene comes storming out from her bedroom, pistol nowhere
in sight. But when she tosses her clutch on the table, it
lands with a THUNK.

                    MARJORIE
         They make lipstick so heavy these
         days.

                    IRENE
         What?

Irene grabs a sewing kit from a drawer and starts to work
on her jacket button.

                    MARJORIE
         What's in the purse? A horse shoe?
         You hoping to get lucky?

                    IRENE
         Do you know how hard it is for a
         woman to carry a concealed weapon?

                    MARJORIE
         Why would a woman need to carry a
         concealed weapon? That's what men
         are for.

                    IRENE
         Lucky? What did you mean by that?
         Who would I -- never mind.
            (MORE)

                    IRENE (CONT'D)
          The point is, a private detective
          never knows when they're going to
          be in a situation that might
          require some...
                    (searching)
          Firepower.

Marjorie raises her eyebrows and sneaks a peek inside the
clutch. Her eyes go wide.

                    MARJORIE
          Irene! You bought a gun? Do you
          even know how to use it?

                    IRENE
          Of course I --

                    MARJORIE
          And since when do detectives'
          secretaries need -- what did you
          call it -- firepower?

Irene snatches her clutch away from Marjorie.

                    IRENE
          I may be nothing more than a
          secretary today. But I can run
          investigative circles around Sig
          Pfefferle. It's just a matter of
          time before --

                    MARJORIE
          He fires you? Face it, honey. Men
          don't like it when other people
          make them feel stupid. Especially
          when "other people" is a woman.

                    IRENE
          I don't need him to like me. I
          just need him to see that I have
          more to offer than typing skills.

                    MARJORIE
          And nice legs.

                    IRENE
          That's not why he hired me. He may
          be dumber than a bucket, but he's
          always been a gentleman.

                    MARJORIE
          Uh-huh.

Marjorie stands and puts her cup and plate in the sink.

                              MARJORIE (CONT'D)
                    If you'll excuse me, I've gotta
                    get beautiful. I actually want my
                    boss to like me. And my legs.


                              IRENE
                    That lug still hasn't proposed?


                              MARJORIE
                    I don't want to talk about it.

She disappears into her bedroom, leaving Irene smiling
and shaking her head.

                                        DISSOLVE TO:


MAGNIFYING GLASS POV

A grainy black-and-white photo of mob boss QUINCY ROMANO
(late 30s), surrounded by goons and lackeys, at the grand
opening of his nightclub, The Pelican. The lens GLIDES
over the photo and STOPS on a curly-haired slob in the
background.


INT. SIG'S OFFICE - RECEPTION - LATE MORNING

Irene hunches over the picture on her desk with a
magnifying glass. She's totally absorbed.

                              SIG (O.S.)
                    Any messages?

Irene nearly jumps out of her skin. She looks up to see
her boss, SIG PFEFFERLE, a balding man in his 40s who
looks more like an accountant than a private detective.

                              IRENE
                    No, Mr. Pfefferle. No messages.

Sig heads for his inner office.

                              IRENE (CONT'D)
                    Mr. Pfefferle.

                              SIG
                    Hmm?

                              IRENE
                    Mr. Pfefferle, have you made any
                    progress on the missing trombone
                    player? Sammy Petruccio?

Sig sighs. This isn't the first of these conversations, and he's getting bored with them.

                    SIG
          Let me guess, you found something.

Irene gets up and hands the photo to him. She points to the curly-haired slob in the background.

                    IRENE
          That's him, isn't it?

                    SIG
          And?

                    IRENE
          And Quincy Romano. The mob boss.

                    SIG
          And?

                    IRENE
          Well... do you think there's a
          connection?

Sig hands the photo back and shoos Irene away.

                    SIG
          Sure, there's a connection. Sammy
          played trombone at a club owned by
          Romano. The club celebrating its
          grand opening in that photograph.
               (mocking)
          Very suspicious, indeed.

                    IRENE
          It is when you consider none of
          the other band members are there.
          Maybe playing in the band wasn't
          the only thing Sammy --

                    SIG
          Miss Granger, you seem to be under
          the impression that I don't know
          how to do my job.

That's exactly the impression she's under, but Irene holds her tongue.

                    SIG (CONT'D)
          These are things I've already
          considered. Leads I've already
          pursued. And they led nowhere.
               (beat)
                    (MORE)

                    SIG (CONT'D)
          Now, perhaps instead of trying to
          do my job, you could do yours and
          get me some coffee.

                    IRENE
          Already on your desk, Mr.
          Pfefferle.

Sig seems irritated that she's a step ahead of him. He
disappears inside his office with a scowl and a DOOR SLAM
for good measure.

                    IRENE (CONT'D)
          Ten to one, he asks the bandleader
          if playing trombone was all Sammy
          did at the club.
                    (answers herself)
          You're on, Miss Granger.
                    (beat)
          Detective Granger?
                    (beat)
          Investigator Granger?

The door to the hallway opens, snapping Irene back to
reality.

DICKIE HUGGINS (30) walks in. He's normally all smiles
and charm, but right now, he looks worried.

                    IRENE (CONT'D)
          Mr. Huggins.

Dickie barely glances at her.

                    DICKIE
          Is Sig in?

                    IRENE
          I'll let him know you're here.

She picks up the phone and flips a switch on the
intercom.

                    IRENE (CONT'D)
          Mr. Pfefferle? Dickie Huggins is
          here to see you.

She sets the phone back in its cradle.

                    IRENE (CONT'D)
          Go right in, Mr. Huggins.

Dickie goes into the inner office.

Irene waits a beat, then tiptoes to the door and presses
an ear against it. The voices are muffled, but she can
hear the whole conversation.

                    SIG (O.S.)
          I told you over the phone I had no
          new information.

                    DICKIE (O.S.)
          Did you talk to Quincy?

INT. SIG'S OFFICE - INNER OFFICE - SAME

Sig sits behind his desk, reading a newspaper, not even
bothering to look at Dickie.

                    SIG
          No reason to.

                    DICKIE
          What about Cornie?

The newspaper comes down.

                    SIG
          Look, Dickie, I'm gonna give it to
          you straight. There's nothing
          here. It's a dead end. Time to
          find yourself a new trombonist.

INT. SIG'S OFFICE - RECEPTION - SAME

Irene's face registers complete surprise.

                    DICKIE (O.S.)
          That's it? You're giving up?

                    SIG (O.S.)
          I told you from the start the note
          Sammy left was probably real. He's
          probably off on some tropical
          island having a good laugh at your
          expense right now. So move on.

A long beat of silence.

                    DICKIE (O.S.)
          How much do I owe you?

Irene doesn't wait to hear the answer. She scurries back
to her desk. Just in time too -- Dickie opens the inner
office door just as she settles into her seat.

Dickie crosses the room to leave.

>                    IRENE
>               (just above a
>                whisper)
>          Mr. Huggins.

Dickie turns.

>                    IRENE (CONT'D)
>          I have a theory about --

Sig comes into the room, cutting Irene off.

>                    IRENE (CONT'D)
>               (normal voice)
>          Good day, Mr. Huggins.

Dickie gives her a curious look, but doesn't give her
away.

>                    DICKIE
>          Good day.

He leaves.


INT. AUTOMAT - EVENING

Irene and Marjorie slide their trays along the counter as
they peruse their dining options.

Marjorie inserts a nickel, lifts a window, and pulls out
a piece of pie.

>                    IRENE
>          Sometimes I wonder if he's really
>          that bad at his job, or if he's
>          just lazy.

Irene chooses something more practical: a slice of
meatloaf.

>                    MARJORIE
>          Mm-hmm.

>                    IRENE
>          There are obvious leads for him to
>          follow, but for some reason... I
>          don't know, maybe he's scared.
>          Quincy Romano is pretty powerful.

>                    MARJORIE
>          Mm-hmm.

They each add a carton of milk to their trays and head
for an open table.

                    IRENE
          And any buffoon could tell that
          note was a fake.


                    MARJORIE
          Mm-hmm.

                    IRENE
          Are you even listening?

Marjorie looks like she's been caught.


                    MARJORIE
          Mm-hmm?


                    IRENE
          Marjorie!

                    MARJORIE
          I have been listening, honest. Mr.
          Pfefferle is lazy and dumb and
          yellow. Did I miss anything?


                    IRENE
          I just know there's more to it.
          And Mr. Huggins -- he's the
          bandleader, the one who hired Mr.
          Pfefferle -- he knows it too. And
          I know I could... If I could
          just... But how? Who's going to
          take a woman detective seriously?

Marjorie shrugs as she stuffs a bite of pie into her
mouth.

                    MARJORIE
          Maybe it's time to move on. Start
          fresh. Find a new line of work.
          Hey, I hear the Pelican is looking
          for a new trombone player.

Irene gives her friend a look that says she's not amused.
But then, an idea begins to dawn:

                    MARJORIE (CONT'D)
          Honestly, honey, I don't know why
          you let Pfefferle get you so
          worked up. It's just a job.

                    IRENE
          The Pelican... that's it.
          Marjorie, you're a genius.

                    MARJORIE
          Yes, I am, thank you. But... why?

                    IRENE
          I could go undercover at the
          Pelican. I can sing... sort of.
          And dance a little. I was always
          the lead in school plays, you
          know. It's perfect.

Irene is elated.


EXT. PELICAN - FRONT - NIGHT

Irene slowly passes the main doors to the Pelican, trying
to get a look inside.

A huge sign out front reads "DICKIE HUGGINS AND HIS
SWINGIN' BAND."


INT. PELICAN - MAIN ROOM - SAME

It's a posh but lively nightclub. A place you'd picture
Fred and Ginger entertaining. Men in dinner jackets.
Women in elegant gowns.

Ladies and gents crowd the broad dance floor in front of
a stage, where Dickie leads the BAND. They PLAY A HOT,
SWINGIN' TUNE.


EXT. PELICAN - BACKSTAGE ENTRANCE - SAME

Irene walks down the alley, heading for the door that
leads backstage.

It's cracked open just a smidge, and the MUSIC FLOATS
OUT.

Irene stops before she reaches the door and takes off her
glasses. It takes a little rearranging, but she manages
to stuff the glasses into her clutch next to the .38
Colt. (From now on, Irene only wears glasses at home and
at the office.)

Just as she reaches for the door handle, the door swings
wide open, nearly taking her out and causing her to drop
her clutch.

A sous chef and a waiter -- GEORGE (20s) -- emerge, lighting up cigarettes.

They catch sight of Irene. The sous chef whistles, and George stares.

Flustered, Irene bends to pick up her clutch, but George beats her to it. He hands it to her and smiles.

Irene blushes and hurries inside.


INT. PELICAN - BACKSTAGE HALLWAY

The MUSIC GROWS LOUDER as Irene makes her way toward the wing of the stage. The MUSIC draws her.

Soon she's standing just offstage, just out of sight of the dancing patrons, watching Dickie lead the band.

She doesn't notice the two gentlemen conversing in hushed tones nearby, but they notice her.

One is a familiar face: Quincy Romano. Suave, debonair, disarming.

The other is Quincy's right hand man, CORNIE MULLOY (30s). He's probably never smiled once in his whole life. Probably doesn't even know how.

Cornie starts toward Irene, but Quincy puts a hand up to stop him. Quincy goes instead.

He whispers in Irene's ear:

                    QUINCY
          Are you enjoying the music?

Irene jumps. Her eyes go wide when she sees his face. But she recovers quickly.

                    IRENE
          I'm here to see Mr. Huggins about
          a job with the band. I'm a singer.

                    QUINCY
          Is Dickie expecting you?

                    IRENE
          Not exactly.

The SONG ENDS, and the PATRONS APPLAUD.

As the band disperses for a set break, Dickie comes trotting offstage. He sees Quincy and Cornie. Recognizes Irene, but can't quite place her.

                    QUINCY
          Dickie, this charming young lady
          would like to audition for the
          Pelican.

                    DICKIE
          Oh?

                    QUINCY
          She sings.

                    IRENE
          And dances.

                    DICKIE
          Really.

                    QUINCY
          How about it, Dickie?

                    DICKIE
          I don't know, Mr. Romano. We don't
          really need a new act.

                    QUINCY
          It wasn't a suggestion.

Dickie blanches.

                    DICKIE
              (to Irene)
          Tomorrow. Noon. Bring your own
          music.

                    IRENE
          Thank you, Mr. Huggins.

Dickie continues on toward his dressing room, casting one last curious glance over his shoulder.

Irene smiles up at Quincy.

He smiles down at her.

                    IRENE (CONT'D)
          And thank you, Mr. Romano.

                    QUINCY
          So you do know who I am.

                         IRENE
          Doesn't everyone?

                         QUINCY
          But I still don't know who you
          are.

                         IRENE
          Miss... LeGrange. Irene LeGrange.

Quincy takes Irene's hand and kisses it. An old-fashioned
gentleman.

                         QUINCY
          A pleasure, Miss LeGrange.


INT. IRENE'S APARTMENT - BEDROOM - NIGHT

Irene stands with her hands on her hips in the middle of
the room, surveying the mess of notes and clippings and
photos all around her.

She shuffles through the mess until she finds a publicity
photo of Dickie and his band.

Even in his performance tux, Sammy the trombonist looks
like a slob.

She kicks around in another pile until she finds a
mugshot of Quincy.

Even being processed by police, Quincy looks debonair.

She compares the two. They couldn't be more different.
And yet...

Irene tosses the pictures on the bed and rummages through
the haphazardly scattered documents. Most she shoves
aside, but every now and then, she tosses one on the bed
with the pictures.


INT. IRENE'S APARTMENT - MARJORIE'S ROOM - EARLY MORNING

Marjorie sprawls on her stomach on her bed, her covers
half on the floor, a plate with crumbs next to one hand.

Irene leans over her and gently shakes her shoulder.

                         IRENE
          Marjorie. Marjorie.

Marjorie startles awake so fast she almost backhands
Irene in the face.

                    MARJORIE
          Plaza-one-double-five-double-four.

                    IRENE
          Marjorie, I need your help.

Marjorie looks surprised.


INT. SIG'S OFFICE - RECEPTION - DAY

The clock on the wall reads 11:45.

Irene has one eye on the clock and one on Sig's door. Her
hair is done up a little fancier today, her outfit a
little more daring, her lipstick a little brighter.

She gathers her courage. Walks to Sig's door. Knocks.

                    SIG (O.S.)
          Come in.

Irene opens the door...


INT. SIG'S OFFICE - INNER OFFICE

Sig is absorbed in paperwork on his desk. He doesn't look
up when Irene pokes her head inside.

                    IRENE
          Mr. Pfefferle?

                    SIG
          Hmm.

                    IRENE
          If it's all right with you, I'll
          take my lunch now.

Sig finally looks up.

                    SIG
          Isn't it a little early for lunch?

Irene is prepared for this question.

                    IRENE
          I thought I'd take a long lunch to
          run some of your errands.

                         SIG
          Long lunch is one thing. But you
          never take an early lunch. What's
          the rush?

                         IRENE
          I want to make sure I'm back for
          your afternoon appointment.

                         SIG
          Oh. Well, hold off, will you? I
          have some letters to finish that I
          want you to post when you go out.

Irene's eyes flick to the clock. 11:48.

                         IRENE
          How long do you think it'll take?
              (belated)
          Mr. Pfefferle?

                         SIG
          As long as it takes.
              (a beat)
          Miss Granger.


                         IRENE
          Yes, sir.

She shuts the door.


INT. SIG'S OFFICE - RECEPTION

Irene plunks down at her desk and taps her foot nervously
as she watches the second hand make its way around the
clock face. 11:50.


INT. PELICAN - MAIN ROOM - SAME

Dickie sits on the edge of the empty stage, feet
dangling. He checks his watch.

His PIANO PLAYER (40) GOOFS AROUND ON THE KEYS, sometimes
playing bits of recognizable melody, but it flows
seamlessly into improv.

Waiters mill about, taking chairs off tables, mopping
floors, polishing silver.

INT. SIG'S OFFICE - RECEPTION - SAME

Irene paces the room now. Glances at the clock. 11:55.

Sig's door opens.

Before Sig can say a word, Irene snatches the letters
from his hand and runs out the door, remembering just in
time to grab her hat and clutch on her way out.


INT. PELICAN - MAIN ROOM - SAME

George comes to sit next to Dickie on the stage.

> GEORGE
> A little early for you fellas,
> isn't it?

> DICKIE
> Holding an audition. A singer.

> GEORGE
> I thought the only singer you'd
> ever put in front of your band was
> you.

> DICKIE
> Yeah, well... we'll see. She may
> not even show up.

He checks his watch again. 12:03.

Suddenly, Irene comes flying into the room from
backstage, one hand on her hat to keep it on her head.
Her hair, so beautiful earlier, is now sticking out in
all directions.

> IRENE
> I'm here, Mr. Huggins! Please tell
> me I'm not too late.

George, Dickie, and the Piano Player turn in surprise.

George's face lights up.

> GEORGE
> Oh, it's you.

Irene gives him a quizzical look.

Dickie draws her attention back:

                         DICKIE
              Did you bring music, Miss...?

                         IRENE
              LeGrange. You can call me Irene.
              Um... no. But I can sightread.

George returns to his work, unnoticed by Dickie and
Irene.

Dickie looks over at the Piano Player, who shakes his
head.

                         PIANO PLAYER
              Everything I got's up here.

He points to his temple.

                         DICKIE
              I'm sorry, Miss LeGrange --

                         IRENE
              I could sing one of your songs,
              Mr. Huggins. I know them all. I
              own every record. Well, nearly
              every one. There was one a couple
              years ago --

                         DICKIE
              That'll be fine, Miss LeGrange.
              Which one would you like to sing
              for us?

                         IRENE
              Oh, um...
                   (thinks)
              "Midnight Promises?"

Dickie nods to the Piano Player, who starts the SLOW
BALLAD INTRO.

Irene sets her hat and clutch aside, calms her breathing
and smooths her hair as the INTRO PLAYS. She closes her
eyes and listens for the BUILD TO HER CUE.

When she sings, it's clear she sold herself short with
Marjorie. Irene has a lovely voice and natural
musicality.

> IRENE (CONT'D)
> HE HAD A TONGUE OF SILVER
> HIS WORDS WERE SPUN WITH GOLD
> OH HOW I WOULD BELIEVE
> ALL THE SPLENDID MIDNIGHT PROMISES
> HE TOLD

Dickie is visibly impressed. He wasn't expecting this.

> IRENE (CONT'D)
> ALL THE THINGS HE TOLD ME
> WERE A CLEVER MASQUERADE
> OH WHY DID I BELIEVE
> ALL THE LOVELY MIDNIGHT PROMISES
> HE MADE

Irene puts her heart and soul into the song.

All around, one by one, the waiters, including George, stop what they're doing and simply listen.

> IRENE (CONT'D)
> HOW COULD I HAVE BEEN SO BLIND
> HOW COULD I FALL SO DEEP
> HOW COULD I HAVE BEEN CONVINCED
> BY PROMISES HE DIDN'T INTEND TO
> KEEP
>
> HE LEFT ME BROKENHEARTED
> BUT HIS KISSES I STILL CRAVE
> I WISH I'D NOT BELIEVED
> ALL THE BROKEN MIDNIGHT PROMISES
> HE GAVE

When the SONG ENDS, no one moves. No one speaks.

The silence and stillness make Irene self-conscious.

> IRENE (CONT'D)
> I'm sorry. I shouldn't have --

> DICKIE
> I must've sung that song a
> thousand times. But I heard
> something in it just now I've
> never heard before.

> IRENE
> Something bad?

Dickie shakes his head and smiles. Suddenly, it comes to him, and he snaps his fingers.

                    DICKIE
          The secretary!

He looks around at the waiters, who are ever so slowly
getting back to their work.

He pulls Irene aside. When he's sure no one else can hear
their conversation:

                    DICKIE (CONT'D)
          You work for Sig. Did he send you?
          I thought he said he wasn't going
          to continue the investigation.

Irene swallows.

                    IRENE
          He's not. But I am.

Dickie looks unsure. But:

                    DICKIE
          I'll hire you to sing -- I'd be a
          fool not to -- but if you're doing
          what I think you're doing... If
          Quincy finds out...

                    IRENE
          Do you mean that?

                    DICKIE
          Yes. He's not a forgiving man.

                    IRENE
          No, I mean what you said about --
          how you'd be a fool not to hire
          me? Was I really okay?

Dickie is surprised. He smiles. Moves in a little closer.

                    DICKIE
          You were magnificent.

Irene takes a half step backward. Clears her throat.

                    IRENE
          Who was that big, dumb-looking
          fellow Quincy had with him last
          night?

                    DICKIE
          Who, Cornie Mulloy?

                    IRENE
          An Irishman?

                    DICKIE
          He's Quincy's puppet. His gofer.
          His fists. Whatever Quincy needs
          him to be, whenever he needs him
          to be it.

Irene takes this in. And then:

                    IRENE
          Magnificent? Really?

Dickie smiles again.

                    DICKIE
          When can you start?


INT. PELICAN - DRESSING ROOM - NIGHT

Irene finds herself once again in front of a full-length
mirror.

Only now, the glasses and tasteful ladies' suit are gone,
replaced by an evening gown with a generous slit in the
skirt and a neckline that makes her blush.

She takes a sheer scarf and tries to position it over her
cleavage. It hides nothing. And it looks ridiculous.

                    IRENE
          What have you gotten yourself into
          this time, Irene? Didn't think
          about what you'd have to wear, did
          you? I'd like to see you try to
          hide a gun in this little number.

A KNOCK on the DOOR.

                    IRENE (CONT'D)
          Come in.

Dickie enters. Admires Irene in the reflection.

Irene turns to him.

He plucks the sheer scarf away from her chest and holds
it up.

                    DICKIE
          What's this?

                    IRENE
          Desperation.

Dickie gives her a puzzled look.

                    IRENE (CONT'D)
          I'm all nerves.

                    DICKIE
          You're going to be great. Because
          you are great.

Irene takes Dickie's hand.

                    IRENE
          Even if I'm not... I promise, Mr.
          Huggins, no matter what, I'm going
          to find out what happened to Sammy
          Petruccio.

Dickie smiles.

                    DICKIE
          You look ravishing, Irene.

It's not the response Irene expected.

Another KNOCK.

                    VOICE (O.S.)
          Five minutes, Mr. Huggins, Miss
          LeGrange.

                    DICKIE
          See you out there.

Dickie leaves Irene to her own nervous thoughts.


INT. PELICAN - MAIN ROOM

The club is packed with suits and skirts, most of them
with a martini glass or champagne flute already half-
drained.

Waiters scurry to and fro with food platters and menus
and drink trays.

The band is assembled on stage, but not yet playing.

Quincy wines and dines his way around the room, stopping
at one table for a moment, ordering a drink at another,
only to move on again after the niceties have been
properly exchanged.

Finally, he makes his way to the microphone at the front of the stage.

> QUINCY
> Ladies and gentlemen. My
> distinguished guests. Welcome to
> my humble establishment.

Some SCATTERED APPLAUSE.

> QUINCY (CONT'D)
> It is with supreme pleasure and
> delight that I present to you this
> evening's entertainment. If you've
> been to the Pelican before, or if
> you've lived in this country for
> more than five minutes, you've no
> doubt heard Mr. Dickie Huggins and
> His Band...

More ENTHUSIASTIC APPLAUSE as Dickie trots on stage and takes up his baton.

> QUINCY (CONT'D)
> But tonight, we present to you a
> new star, a sparkling jewel
> plucked from the heavens by my
> very own hand. Ladies and
> gentlemen, Miss Irene LeGrange.

The lights dim as Quincy exits and Dickie counts off.

The DRUMS RAP OUT A HOT TEMPO for eight bars before the DOUBLE BASS JOINS.

The PIANO COMES IN next, then the BRASS and SAXOPHONES. Suddenly, as it BUILDS TO A CLIMAX, it all comes to a SCREECHING HALT.

A spotlight hits stage right, and Irene steps -- or rather trips -- into it from behind the curtain. A communal GASP comes from the AUDIENCE, but she recovers.

A beat.

Irene starts slowly, a cappella, and as the INSTRUMENTS SNEAK IN under her, the song becomes a leisurely seduction.

And it's working. The audience is entranced.

                         IRENE
              YOU SAW YOUR CHANCE
              AND RIGHT ON CUE
              YOU STOLE A GLANCE
              YOU SCOUNDREL YOU


JUST OFFSTAGE

Quincy watches Irene with ravenous eyes.

                         IRENE
              YOU COULDN'T MISS
              YOUR CHANCE TO WOO
              YOU STOLE A KISS
              YOU SCOUNDREL YOU


AT THE BAR

George waits for a drink order, but he can't tear his
gaze from Irene.

                         IRENE
              I DID MY BEST TO PROTEST
              BUT YOU KNEW IT WAS IN JEST
              I COULD SEE WHAT WOULD BE
              IF I LET YOU CAPTURE ME

The bartender sets a couple of cocktails on George's
drink tray.

George doesn't notice. Unable to help himself, he takes a
seat on the nearest barstool and enjoys the performance.

                      IRENE (CONT'D)
              YOU PLAYED IT SMART
              KNEW WHAT TO DO
              YOU STOLE MY HEART
              YOU SCOUNDREL YOU


ON STAGE

Dickie smiles back over his shoulder at Irene. They make
eye contact for a brief moment, and he winks at her.

Irene pretends not to notice.

                              IRENE
                I DID MY BEST TO PROTEST
                BUT YOU KNEW IT WAS IN JEST
                I COULD SEE WHAT WOULD BE
                IF I LET YOU CAPTURE ME

                YOU PLAYED IT SMART
                KNEW WHAT TO DO
                YOU STOLE MY HEART
                YOU SCOUNDREL YOU

The SONG ENDS, and the CLUB ERUPTS in RAUCOUS APPLAUSE.


AT THE BAR

Several patrons cast dirty looks at George, still staring
dreamily from his barstool.

Without seeming to realize what he's doing, he grabs the
nearest cocktail -- one belonging to a BESPECTACLED
CUSTOMER (50) -- and sips on it.

                    BESPECTACLED CUSTOMER
                Hey!

The bartender grabs the drink out of George's hand and
jerks his head toward the tables.

George comes back to reality and jumps off the barstool.
He nods apologetically to the Bespectacled Customer and
the other surly patrons.

                              GEORGE
                I beg your pardon. Weak knees.
                It's hereditary.

He rushes away as the bartender hands the Bespectacled
Customer a new cocktail.

A beat later George returns to retrieve his drink tray,
accidentally bumping into the Bespectacled Customer and
sloshing his cocktail all over.

George ducks and runs before the Bespectacled Customer
can figure out what hit him.


INT. PELICAN - BACKSTAGE HALLWAY - LATER

Irene steps into the hallway from her dressing room,
comfortably back in her ladies' suit.

The LEAD TRUMPET (30s) and BARI SAX (20s) players pass her, instrument cases in hand.

> LEAD TRUMPET
> Good night, Miss LeGrange.

> BARI SAX
> You slaughtered 'em. Can't wait to
> do it again tomorrow night.

Irene smiles.

> IRENE
> Good night, fellas.

Once they are out of sight, Irene takes a cautious step toward another dressing room. Pokes her head inside.

> GEORGE (O.S.)
> Forget which one is yours?

Irene jumps. When she turns to see George watching her with amusement, she frowns.

> IRENE
> Oh. You.

> GEORGE
> That's rude.

Irene rolls her eyes and heads for the exit.

George rushes to get to the door first so he can hold it open for her.

Irene tries really hard to be annoyed by the gesture, but it's kinda cute.


EXT. PELICAN - BACKSTAGE ENTRANCE

They step outside and begin an unhurried walk, side-by-side down the alleyway.

> IRENE
> You're a waiter here, right?

> GEORGE
> For now. Name's George.

> IRENE
> Did you know the trombone player
> who used to be here? Sammy?

                              GEORGE
                    Sure. Why? Do you know him too?

                              IRENE
                    What do you mean, for now? Do you
                    have bigger plans?

                              GEORGE
                    Oh, sure. I'm gonna run the joint
                    someday. Do you know Sammy well?
                    Are you two...

They turn onto...


EXT. STREET

If it weren't 3 AM, it would be a busy thoroughfare. But
just now, it's only the two of them.

                              IRENE
                    What? No. I don't even know Sammy.

                              GEORGE
                    Then why'd you ask if I know him?

Irene realizes her mistake and rushes to cover.

                              IRENE
                    What I mean is, I hardly know him.
                    We played a gig together once. And
                    I had heard somewhere that he was
                    playing with Dickie's band now,
                    but he wasn't there tonight. Maybe
                    I heard wrong.

George looks like he's not really buying it, but he
doesn't press her on it.

                              GEORGE
                    I heard he cracked his nut and ran
                    off to start a new life.

                              IRENE
                    When you say "run the joint"... Do
                    you mean buy it? Buy the Pelican?

                              GEORGE
                    When you say you "played a gig
                    together"... Is that a euphemism?

Irene is shocked and offended. Stops in her tracks.

George stops too.

Too upset to speak, Irene turns on her heel to walk away.

But George grabs her wrist and twirls her...

                    GEORGE (CONT'D)
          IRENE

                    IRENE
          Miss LeGrange, if you please.

                    GEORGE
          DON'T BE MEAN, IRENE
          OR CAUSE A SCENE, IRENE
          THERE'S SOMETHING BETWEEN
               US

                    IRENE
          THERE'S NOTHING BETWEEN
               US

It's a cat-and-mouse NUMBER. She walks away, he twirls
her back. He tries to pull her close, she ducks and spins
away.

                    GEORGE
          WHY DO YOU INSIST ON RESISTING
          THIS CHEMISTRY WE FEEL

                    IRENE
          WHY DO YOU PERSIST WITH EXISTING
          IN A WORLD THAT ISN'T REAL

Benches, fire hydrants, lampposts, collection mailboxes,
telephone booths... they're all props and obstacles that
sometimes create space between Irene and George, and
sometimes bring them closer.

                    GEORGE
          WHAT CAN I DO TO PERSUADE YOU
          TO GIVE THIS THING A TRY

                    IRENE
          WHAT CAN I DO TO EVADE YOU
          WHAT YOU'RE SELLING I WON'T BUY

Even though Irene persists in evading, George is winning
her over with every move.

                    GEORGE
          IRENE
          YOU'RE A QUEEN, IRENE
          LET'S CONVENE, IRENE
          CAN'T YOU SEE WHAT'S BETWEEN
               US

                         IRENE
                   WHAT'S BETWEEN US

Irene dances up some apartment steps.

George follows her. Gets in front of her.

She slides down the rail.

He leaps back to the sidewalk.

She runs up the steps again and reaches the door this
time, but he grabs her wrist and turns her back to face
him.

                         GEORGE
              WHEN WILL YOU END THIS PRETENDING
              CONCEDE THAT YOU WERE WRONG
              WHEN WILL YOU BEND TO THIS
                    BLENDING
              CONFESS THAT WE BELONG

The MUSIC SLOWS as her hands slide up to grip his lapel
and pull him close.

                         GEORGE (CONT'D)
              IRENE
              YOU'RE A QUEEN, IRENE
              LET'S CONVENE, IRENE
              CAN'T YOU SEE WHAT'S BETWEEN
                    US

                         IRENE
              THERE COULD BE SOMETHING BETWEEN
                    US

Just before their lips meet, she shoves him backwards and
races inside.

The DOOR CLICKS SHUT by the time George recovers.

He smiles. Slides down the rail and trudges down the
sidewalk, hands in his pockets. He whistles the melody as
he glances back at her apartment door one more time.


INT. IRENE'S APARTMENT - SAME

Irene slips inside the door, humming the last bars of the
tune. She leans back against it and smiles to herself.

                                        DISSOLVE TO:

INT. SIG'S OFFICE - RECEPTION - MORNING

Irene yawns as she enters and flicks on the lights. She
looks beat.

She sets her hat and clutch -- THUNK -- on her desk and
goes to the file cabinet.

She opens the drawer labeled "O-S" and flips through file
folders until she finds the one named "Petruccio, Samuel
R." She pulls it out.

At her desk, she sits and opens the folder.

It's empty except for the note Sammy supposedly left
behind.

                    IRENE
          Sheesh. I knew he was lazy, but...

She studies the letter:

"Dickie,

Hate to leave you in the lurch, but I'm through with the
band. Don't bother trying to track me down. I don't want
to be found.

Sammy P."

Irene turns the letter over, looking for something.
Anything.

She considers... and writes herself a list as she talks
it through with herself.

                    IRENE (CONT'D)
          First order of business: verify
          that this is Sammy's handwriting.
                    (beat)
          Second, if it is, find out why he
          wanted to leave the band. Was it
          about money? Was he through with
          music? Or with whatever work he
          was doing for Quincy?
                    (beat)
          Third --

The door opens, and Sig walks in.

Irene flips her list facedown and jumps up.

                    IRENE (CONT'D)
          Good morning, Mr. Pfefferle.

> SIG
> Coffee.

> IRENE
> Right away, sir.

Just before Sig disappears into this office:

> IRENE (CONT'D)
> Mr. Pfefferle?

He turns wearily.

> SIG
> What is it, Miss Granger?

> IRENE
> I was doing some filing this
> morning and noticed that your case
> notes are missing from Sammy
> Petruccio's file. All that's in
> there is the letter he left.

Sig's eyes narrow. It's hard to tell if he's suspicious
or annoyed.

> SIG
> I left my case notes at home.

He turns to go into his office, but pauses for a beat.

> SIG (CONT'D)
> You look tired this morning, Miss
> Granger. It's unbecoming.

And he shuts the door.


EXT. PELICAN - FRONT - EVENING

Irene passes the main doors and notes with a little bit
of pride and pleasure that the sign out front now has a
white strip that reads "Feat. Irene LeGrange" pasted just
underneath the band's billing.


EXT. PELICAN - BACKSTAGE ENTRANCE

Irene hurries down the alley toward the backstage door.

> DICKIE (O.S.)
> Irene! Wait up!

Irene turns to see Dickie paying off a cab where the alley dumps onto the street.

He jogs to catch up and falls into step beside her.

> IRENE
> I'm glad to see you, Mr. Huggins --

> DICKIE
> Please, call me Dickie. And I'm glad to see you too.

He means it differently than she does.

> IRENE
> I have so many questions I want to ask you.

Dickie opens the backstage door for her. She enters, and he follows...

INT. PELICAN - BACKSTAGE HALLWAY

Dickie hovers at Irene's shoulder as she walks.

> DICKIE
> I have some things I want to ask you too. What do you say we have a little rehearsal tomorrow, just you and me, work in some new numbers, then I can treat you to lunch?

> IRENE
> Without the band?

> DICKIE
> I want to be sure the songs work for you before I get the band involved.

> IRENE
> Oh. Okay. And I can ask you all my questions then?

> DICKIE
> You can ask me anything you want then.

He kisses her on the forehead and leaves her at her dressing room door.

Irene frowns and rubs her forehead.

INT. PELICAN - DRESSING ROOM

Irene is surprised to find someone in her dressing room:
Quincy. She recovers and turns on the charm.

>                    IRENE
>          Mr. Romano. You scared me half to
>          death.

Quincy kisses her hand. Ever the gentleman.

>                    QUINCY
>          Please forgive me. I wanted to
>          make sure I caught you before you
>          went on tonight. You see, I
>          haven't had a chance to tell you
>          what a revelation you are. My
>          patrons can't stop talking about
>          you. And I can't blame them.

>                    IRENE
>          You're too kind.

>                    QUINCY
>          I wonder, Miss LeGrange, if you
>          would do me the honor -- the very
>          great honor -- of spending the day
>          with me tomorrow?

>                    IRENE
>          Oh, Mr. Romano, I am sorry. Truly.
>          But I've just made plans to
>          rehearse some new numbers with Mr.
>          Huggins tomorrow.

>                    QUINCY
>          Sunday, then?

>                    IRENE
>          It would be a pleasure.

He kisses her hand again.

>                    QUINCY
>          I shall count the hours.

Irene smiles as he leaves. But once he's gone, she wipes
the back of her hand on her skirt.


INT. PELICAN - BACKSTAGE HALLWAY - LATER

Dressed for her number, Irene comes out of her dressing
room and nearly bumps into George.

                         IRENE
              Oh. You.

She's trying hard to be annoyed, but a smile plays at the
corners of her mouth.

                         GEORGE
              You're about to go on?

                         IRENE
              Yeah, I've got about thirty
              seconds before Quincy -- Mr.
              Romano -- introduces me.

Irene heads down the hall.

George follows her.

                         GEORGE
              Then I'll be quick. Can I walk you
              home again tonight?

                         IRENE
              "Chase" is more like it.

                         GEORGE
              If you'd rather.

Irene laughs. She's about to respond, but Quincy's voice
from the stage interrupts:

                         QUINCY (O.S.)
              ... the city's newest and
              brightest star, Miss Irene
              LeGrange.

Irene rushes away and throws the answer over her
shoulder:

                         IRENE
              Yes!

George smiles.


INT. PELICAN - STAGE

The BAND PLAYS AN UPBEAT TUNE as Irene walks confidently
on stage.

                          IRENE
          YOU'RE SWEET
          A REAL TREAT
          SUGAR, I COULD EAT
          YOU UP

Within the FIRST VERSE, Irene spots Quincy and Cornie
sitting at a table right up front, just at the edge of
the dance floor.

                          IRENE (CONT'D)
          I COULD GO FOR YOU, SUGAR
          SUGAR, I COULD GO FOR YOU

She makes her way down the stairs to the dance floor. She
goes from table to table, directing the flirtatious
lyrics playfully to individual customers.

                          IRENE (CONT'D)
          THIS COULD BE STICKY
          A LITTLE TRICKY
          BUT, HONEY, I AIN'T PICKY
          'BOUT THAT
          I COULD GO FOR YOU, HONEY
          HONEY, I COULD GO FOR YOU

When she gets to Quincy and Cornie's table, she tickles
Quincy's chin and then sits on Cornie's lap.

                          IRENE (CONT'D)
          IS THIS JUST A GUILTY PLEASURE
          A MINOR FLIRTATION
          OR WILL YOU BE MY TREASURE
          MY LASTING ELATION

Aware of the spotlight, Quincy keeps a smile plastered on
his face, but his eyes shoot daggers at Cornie, who
scowls but does nothing to remove Irene from his lap.

                          IRENE (CONT'D)
          YOU'RE A DOLL
          AND SO TALL
          BABY, I WANNA FALL
          IN LOVE
          I COULD GO FOR YOU, BABY
          BABY, I COULD GO FOR YOU

Irene moves on, and as soon as darkness returns to their
table, Cornie gets up and leaves.

                    IRENE (CONT'D)
          IS THIS JUST A GUILTY PLEASURE
          A MINOR FLIRTATION
          OR WILL YOU BE MY TREASURE
          MY LASTING ELATION

          YOU'RE A DOLL
          AND SO TALL
          BABY, I WANNA FALL
          IN LOVE
          I COULD GO FOR YOU, BABY
          BABY, I COULD GO FOR YOU

Irene mounts the stage as the FINAL VERSE FINISHES WITH A
FLOURISH.

The APPLAUSE is ENTHUSIASTIC as Irene curtsies and exits
stage right.


INT. PELICAN - BACKSTAGE HALLWAY

Cornie takes Irene by surprise. He grabs her shoulders
and shoves her against the wall.

                    IRENE
          Take your hands off me!

She struggles against his hold, but his grip only
tightens until she gasps in pain.

                    CORNIE
          Never do that again.

                    IRENE
          Do what?

                    CORNIE
          I don't need Mr. Romano gettin'
          the wrong idea about you and me,
          hear? He don't like other Joes
          movin' in on his turf, see?

                    IRENE
          His turf?

                    CORNIE
          You stay away from me.

He gives her a last shove before he disappears down the
hallway, leaving Irene shaken.

But her mind is already working.

EXT. PELICAN - BACKSTAGE ENTRANCE - LATER

George paces outside the door, waiting.

Finally, Irene emerges.

George offers Irene his arm, but she walks right past
him. He follows a couple paces behind her.

> GEORGE
> So I'm chasing you home tonight?

> IRENE
> Did Sammy have a girl?

> GEORGE
> George. My name is George. Not
> Sammy. George is walking you home.

> IRENE
> Do you know or don't you?

They turn onto...

EXT. STREET

Irene stops and looks around. Makes sure no one is
watching. Then she loops her arm through George's.

> IRENE
> Well?

> GEORGE
> Why are you so interested in
> Sammy? I thought you hardly knew
> him.

> IRENE
> Why are you not interested? Don't
> you find his disappearance at all
> strange?

> GEORGE
> What business is it of mine if a
> guy wants to do something new with
> his life?

> IRENE
> You aren't even curious?

They stop at a bench and sit.

                    GEORGE
          Sure, I'm curious. But not about
          Sammy. I want to know about Irene
          LeGrange.

                    IRENE
          George. I like that name.

                    GEORGE
          I like you.

He brushes his lips against her cheek. Her neck.

She struggles to keep her train of thought.

                    IRENE
          What about Quincy? Did he have a
          girl before I -- before?

                    GEORGE
               (between kisses)
          Mr. Romano? How should I know?
          He's not exactly chummy with his
          wait staff.

He nuzzles her ear.

She nearly swoons. But then:

                    IRENE
          George, there's something you
          should know.

                    GEORGE
          Tell me.

He plants the softest, briefest kiss on her lips.

Her train of thought is completely gone now.

                    IRENE
          I like you too.

George smiles and draws her in for a real kiss this time.

SOMEONE CLEARS HIS THROAT O.S.

George and Irene break their kiss and stare up at a beat
cop looming over them with his arms crossed.

George tips his hat to the cop, stands, and helps Irene
to her feet.

                              GEORGE
              I beg your pardon, officer. We
              were just... we'll be going now.

Irene tugs him along, and hand-in-hand they run down the
street, giggling like lovestruck teenagers.


INT. PELICAN - MAIN ROOM - DAY

Dickie PLAYS A SIMPLE ACCOMPANIMENT on the PIANO as Irene
sings, reading the sheet music over Dickie's shoulder.

It's a beautiful love song, but we only catch the last
verse.

                              IRENE
              YOUR LOVE IS A SEAL UPON MY HEART
              NEVER TO PART
              PLEASE TELL THAT IT'S TRUE
              FOREVERMORE IT'S ME AND YOU
              THAT THIS IS FOREVER

When it's over, Dickie spins around on the piano bench
and takes Irene's hands in his own.

                              DICKIE
              What do you think? Do you like it?

                              IRENE
              It's beautiful, Dickie. Truly.

                              DICKIE
              I wrote it for you.

Irene disengages her hands and moves away.

                              IRENE
              Goodness. What a lovely
              compliment.

                              DICKIE
              Irene, I told you I had something
              I wanted to ask you --

                              IRENE
              That's right. And I had some
              questions for you. About Sammy.
              And Quincy. And Cornie.

Dickie moves with surprising speed to take Irene in his
arms.

                         DICKIE
          How can you be thinking about
          solving cases at a time like this?
          Don't you realize --

Irene pushes gently away.

                         IRENE
          For instance, do you have a sample
          of Sammy's handwriting? And do you
          know if he had a girl?

Dickie sighs.

                         DICKIE
          No and no.

                         IRENE
          No, he didn't have a girl? Or no,
          you don't know?

                         DICKIE
          No, I don't know. I didn't know
          Sammy that well, truth be told.

                         IRENE
          Then why hire a P-I to find him?
          Are good trombone players so hard
          to come by?

Dickie's mood goes from amorous to irritated.

                         DICKIE
          It's complicated.

                         IRENE
          Do you want me to find out what
          happened to him or not?

                         DICKIE
          Of course, I do.

                         IRENE
          Then un-complicate it for me.

                         DICKIE
          I don't know how he did it, or
          why, but I know it was Quincy. And
          I want to see him face the
          consequences. Just once.

                         IRENE
          If Quincy goes to jail... Wouldn't
          that put you out of a job?

                    DICKIE
          This job, sure. But Dickie Huggins
          and His Band are in high demand.
          Only Quincy's got exclusive
          rights. And a cut of every record
          we sell.

As pieces come together in her head, Irene's face
registers disgust and disbelief.

                    IRENE
          You don't actually care what
          happened to Sammy at all, do you?

                    DICKIE
          Irene, please --

                    IRENE
          No. You were just looking for a
          way to get out of a contract you
          were too dumb or too greedy to say
          no to.

                    DICKIE
          That's not --

                    IRENE
          I have to go.

Irene hurries toward the exit.

Dickie calls out after her:

                    DICKIE
          This doesn't mean you're quitting
          the band, does it?

The DOOR SLAMS.


EXT. PARK - AFTERNOON

Irene and Marjorie stroll through the park.

Marjorie licks an ice cream cone.

Irene is irate.

                    IRENE
          What if Mr. Pfefferle was right
          all along?
                    (MORE)

                    IRENE (CONT'D)
Maybe the note is real, and Sammy
ran off to start a new life, and I
got duped into investigating a
fake case so that a money-grubbing
bandleader doesn't have to share
his profits with his employer.

                    MARJORIE
So quit.

                    IRENE
But what if Sammy really did
disappear? What if Quincy really
is behind some sinister plot to
get rid of Dickie's trombone
player?

                    MARJORIE
So keep going.

                    IRENE
Somehow, the more I find out, the
less I know.

                    MARJORIE
What have you found out?

                    IRENE
That Dickie is a liar, Quincy is
possessive, and George is
insufferable.

                    MARJORIE
You sound more like a woman with
three suitors than a detective
with three suspects.

                    IRENE
They're not suspects. Or suitors.
Well, Quincy is. A suspect, I
mean. At least I think he's still
a suspect. I'm not so sure
anymore. Maybe I can find out more
tomorrow. I'm supposed to spend
the day with him.

                    MARJORIE
Mm-hmm. But he's not a suitor.

                    IRENE
Dickie seemed so sure Quincy was
behind everything, though.

                    MARJORIE
          Dickie the Liar.

                    IRENE
          And it does seem like too obvious
          a connection not to follow it up.
          I mean, he's a mob boss. And
          Cornie...
                    (shivers
                     involuntarily)
          I wonder if his face came out that
          way. Maybe it runs in the family.
          Or maybe --

Irene stops dead in her tracks, eyes wide. She grabs
Marjorie's arm, jarring her ice cream from its cone --
SPLAT -- onto the sidewalk.

Marjorie regards the fallen treat sadly, but Irene
doesn't notice.

                    IRENE (CONT'D)
          Marjorie, that's it! Sammy and
          Quincy are related. Sammy wasn't
          just a musician at Quincy's club.
          He was a member of Quincy's mob
          because he was a member of
          Quincy's family.

Irene throws up a hand to hail a cab.

                    MARJORIE
          Where are you going?

A cab pulls over and Irene leans down to the window.

                    IRENE
          The Municipal Building, please.
                    (to Marjorie)
          Sorry about your ice cream.

She climbs into the cab and rides away.


EXT. PIER - JUST BEFORE DAWN

George and Irene walk arm-in-arm toward the end of the
pier.

Irene detours to the side and leans over the rail. She
shivers, and George takes off his jacket and drapes it
over her shoulders.

Irene absentmindedly hums Dickie's love song.

                    GEORGE
          What's that?

                    IRENE
          Just a song Dickie wrote for m--
          for the band. Would you like to
          hear it?

George nods.

Irene sings it for him.

Hearing it in its entirety, and hearing her sing it for
George... it's a whole different experience than the
rehearsal.

                    IRENE (CONT'D)
          YOUR LOVE IS TEACHING ME TO SEE
          WHO I CAN BE
          I'M DROPPING MY DISGUISE
          BECAUSE I SEE IT IN YOUR EYES
          THAT THIS IS FOREVER

          YOUR LOVE'S LIKE TAKING MY FIRST
               BREATH
          STRONGER THAN DEATH
          I'M CERTAIN YOU'LL DECLARE
          BECAUSE I'M WILLING NOW TO SWEAR
          THAT THIS IS FOREVER

          I NEVER WOULD HAVE GUESSED IT
          THAT I COULD BE SO IN LOVE
          BUT NOW THAT I'VE CONFESSED IT
          I'VE NEVER BEEN SO CERTAIN OF

          YOUR LOVE IS A SEAL UPON MY HEART
          NEVER TO PART
          PLEASE TELL ME THAT IT'S TRUE
          FOREVERMORE IT'S ME AND YOU
          THAT THIS IS FOREVER

                    GEORGE
          I NEVER WOULD HAVE GUESSED IT
          THAT I COULD BE SO IN LOVE
          BUT NOW THAT I'VE CONFESSED IT
          I'VE NEVER BEEN SO CERTAIN OF

                    IRENE
          YOUR LOVE IS A SEAL UPON MY HEART
          NEVER TO PART

                    GEORGE
          PLEASE TELL ME THAT IT'S TRUE
          FOREVERMORE IT'S ME AND YOU

GEORGE AND IRENE
THAT THIS IS FOREVER

As the LAST NOTES FADE OUT, the first rays of sunlight spill over the horizon.

George puts an arm around Irene, and she leans into his shoulder, and they watch the sunrise.


EXT. MARINA - DAY

Quincy steps out of the backseat of a town car and then turns to help Irene out.

In front of them, bobbing in the water, are dozens of yachts of all sizes.

Irene's eyes widen as Quincy leads her to a huge luxury yacht named "La Fortuna è Mobile."

                    IRENE
          What does it mean?

                    QUINCY
          Fortune is fickle.

He stands aside and allows her onto the gangway first.

                    IRENE
          It's marvelous.

At the top of the gangway, Cornie waits with hands stuffed into his trench coat pockets. He wears a scowl as always but refuses to make eye contact with Irene as she passes.

                    QUINCY
               (to Cornie)
          I'm going to give Miss LeGrange a
          little tour, and then we'll be
          lunching on the upper deck. You'll
          see that everything is ready?

                    CORNIE
          Yes, Mr. Romano.

Cornie disappears through a door.

Quincy turns to Irene and smiles.

INT. YACHT - GUEST SUITE - DAY

Quincy opens the door, and Irene peeks inside. She gulps when she sees the bed.

                    QUINCY
          Go on.

Irene cautiously steps inside.

Quincy follows her and the DOOR CLICKS SHUT.

Irene jumps.

                    IRENE
          Mr. Romano --

                    QUINCY
          You must think me impertinent
          showing you a bedroom. But you
          see, this is the closest powder
          room to the upper deck where we
          will be eating. I thought it best
          if I showed it to you now rather
          than attempt to give you
          directions later.

Quincy reaches into the bathroom and flicks on the light.

                    QUINCY (CONT'D)
          See? Come, let us continue.

They leave the suite...


INT. YACHT - PASSAGEWAY

Quincy leads Irene through the narrow passageway.

                    IRENE
          Do you often have guests on board?

                    QUINCY
          Only family, really.

                    IRENE
          Family?

                    QUINCY
          Yes, and even then, not very
          often. But you, my sweet songbird,
          are most welcome to grace one of
          La Fortuna's guest suites any time
          you please.

Irene looks alarmed, about to protest, but Quincy jumps
to reassure her:

                    QUINCY (CONT'D)
          Oh, I mean nothing untoward, Miss
          LeGrange. I pride myself on being
          a gentleman of virtue and
          chivalry. Your honor would be in
          no danger, I assure you.

                    IRENE
          Then I thank you for the offer.

They pass another door in the passageway.

                    IRENE (CONT'D)
          Is this another guest suite? Does
          it look very much like the other
          one?

She reaches for the doorknob, but Quincy blocks her.

                    QUINCY
          That? No, that is my private
          study. Forgive me if I seem
          secretive, but it is not part of
          our tour. Every man needs a sacred
          space, a place no one else may
          enter. You understand, don't you,
          my dear?

                    IRENE
          Of course.

Irene casts a last look over her shoulder as she follows
Quincy to the stairway at the end of the passageway.


EXT. YACHT - UPPER DECK - LATER

Quincy and Irene finish their meal at a table for two,
complete with a champagne bucket and a flower
centerpiece.

                    IRENE
          What a delightful way to spend a
          day. How can I ever thank you?

                    QUINCY
          Join me again tomorrow?

                    IRENE
          You must have more important
          things to do than entertain me day
          after day.

Quincy sighs.

                    QUINCY
          Not more important, but necessary
          nevertheless. Next weekend, then?

Irene merely smiles. She pushes her chair back and
stands.

                    IRENE
          Will you excuse me? I think I'll
          use that powder room.

Her clutch remains resting on the table.


INT. YACHT - GUEST SUITE

Irene slips inside, but she doesn't go to the bathroom.
Instead, she goes first to one bedside table, then the
other, rummaging through the drawers.

Empty.

She opens the wardrobe. Nothing there either.


INT. YACHT - PASSAGEWAY

Irene tiptoes up to the door to Quincy's private study.
Tries the handle. It's locked.

Looking from side to side to make sure no one is coming,
Irene removes her brooch and uses the pin to pick the
lock.

The door swings open...


INT. YACHT - STUDY

Irene hurries inside and eases the door shut. She feels
on either side of the door until she finds the light
switch and flicks it on.

The study is tidy, but lavish. Much like Quincy himself.

Irene rounds the desk and pulls open the top drawer. There's a checkbook and a bundle of cash, but nothing else.

Next drawer down. A stack of papers and a datebook.

Irene flips through the datebook and finds several pages noting appointments with "S.P."

                    IRENE
          Three times a week. Sheesh.
          Whatever he had Sammy doing, it
          must have been very important.

She returns the datebook to its place and moves on to the bottom drawer, deeper than the other two. Only an expensive bottle of scotch, half full, and two whiskey glasses.

FOOTSTEPS IN THE PASSAGEWAY startle her. Irene looks around frantically for a weapon.


EXT. YACHT - UPPER DECK - SAME

Her clutch, with her gun inside, sits on the table.


INT. YACHT - STUDY - SAME

The door handle turns.

Irene dives under the desk just in time.

Cornie pokes his head inside.


UNDER THE DESK

Irene's eyes widen when she sees a Tommy Gun strapped to the underside of the desk.

She adjusts silently -- something underneath her is poking.

She pulls a cigarette case with the initials "S.P." from underneath her.


AT THE DOOR

Cornie seems disturbed that the light is on.

He steps inside and rounds the desk.

UNDER THE DESK

Irene pulls her limbs in as tight as possible as Cornie's SHOES come INTO VIEW in front of her.

She can hear DRAWERS OPENING and PAPERS SHUFFLING.

Finally, the shoes step away, the light goes out, and she hears the DOOR OPEN, CLOSE, and LOCK.

Irene breathes a sigh of relief.


EXT. PELICAN - BACKSTAGE ENTRANCE - EVENING

Quincy's town car rolls down the narrow alley and stops near the backstage door.

Quincy gets out first, then offers a hand to Irene.

> QUINCY
> A more divine day with a more
> charming companion is beyond my
> imagination. Thank you, my dear.

> IRENE
> I should be the one thanking you.

Quincy holds her fingers lightly in his own and pulls her ever so gently toward him.

> QUINCY
> May I?

Before Irene can answer, Quincy bends to kiss her on the cheek.

> QUINCY (CONT'D)
> Ow!

Quincy jerks back, rubbing just above his eyebrow. He laughs as he reaches up and pulls out Irene's hatpin. He holds it in front of her face.

> QUINCY (CONT'D)
> It seems you have hidden weapons.

Irene laughs and takes the hatpin from him.

> IRENE
> So it would seem.

Quincy opts for kissing her hand this time.

                         QUINCY
              I'm afraid I have important
              business to attend to tonight and
              won't be able to see you perform.
              Forgive me?

                         IRENE
              Don't be silly.

Quincy climbs back into the town car.

It drives away.

Irene looks thoughtfully at the hatpin in her hand.


INT. IRENE'S APARTMENT - NIGHT

Irene stands in the middle of the room, arms at her side,
facing the door, concentrating.

She touches her hair gingerly, feeling for something.

Assured, she resumes her stance with her arms at her
side. Rolls her shoulders to relax, prepare, focus.

Suddenly, her hand whips up and pulls a fistful of hair
out of her updo with the hatpin.

                         IRENE
              Ouch!

Undeterred, she hastily puts her hair back up and slides
the hatpin back in, leaving just the tip exposed. Assumes
her stance once more. Like a gunfighter ready to draw.

Her hand whips up again, and this time the hatpin comes
out clean.

She looks at it, satisfied with herself.

She puts the hatpin back and assumes the stance again.

This time, she pulls the hatpin out and flicks her wrist
to throw it like a knife.

But her timing is off. The HATPIN BOUNCES a couple feet
in front of her.

The door opens, and Marjorie comes in with a half-eaten
cotton candy as Irene stoops to retrieve the hatpin.

                         MARJORIE
              Do you ever sleep? It's four in
              the morning.

Irene replaces the hatpin in her hair.

                         IRENE
              Says the girl just coming home
              from...

Marjorie grins and stuffs a chunk of cotton candy in her
mouth.

                         MARJORIE
              He proposed. Well, almost. He said
              he couldn't live without me, which
              is practically the same thing.

                         IRENE
              Stand back.

Marjorie steps aside.

                         MARJORIE
              What are you doing?

                         IRENE
              Only men can carry concealed
              weapons, eh? Watch this.

Irene whips out the hatpin and flicks her wrist.

It's actually a pretty good throw. But it bounces off the
door and falls to the ground.

                         IRENE (CONT'D)
              Shoot!

                         MARJORIE
              Probably not the best thing to say
              if you get in a gunfight with only
              a hatpin to defend you.

Irene picks up the hatpin and inspects it. It's getting a
little bent.

                         IRENE
              Did he give you a ring?

                         MARJORIE
              Only on the Ameche.

                         IRENE
              Then it wasn't a proposal.

Irene unbends the hatpin.

> MARJORIE
> How would you know? Have you ever
> been proposed to?

> IRENE
> (to herself)
> Plenty sharp, but needs to be
> thicker. Stronger.
> (to Marjorie)
> No proposals. Only propositions.

Marjorie raises a single curious eyebrow, but Irene is
too focused on the hatpin to notice.


INT. SIG'S OFFICE - RECEPTION - DAY

Irene leans against the file cabinet, elbow propped on
top and her chin resting in her hand. She dozes.

> SIG'S VOICE
> (on intercom)
> Miss Granger!

Irene startles awake. Dashes to the desk. Presses the
intercom button.

> IRENE
> Yes, Mr. Pfefferle?

> SIG'S VOICE
> (on intercom)
> More coffee.

> IRENE
> Right away, sir.

Irene puts a hand to her forehead and closes her eyes.

> IRENE (CONT'D)
> Better make that two coffees, Miss
> Granger.
> (answers herself)
> Right away, Miss LeGrange.


INT. PELICAN - STAGE - NIGHT

Irene and the BAND GO TO TOWN on Dickie's love song.

                         IRENE
          YOUR LOVE'S LIKE TAKING MY FIRST
              BREATH
          STRONGER THAN DEATH
          I'M CERTAIN YOU'LL DECLARE
          BECAUSE I'M WILLING NOW TO SWEAR
          THAT THIS IS FOREVER

Irene sees a waiter, FRANK, addressing Quincy at his
table. Cornie stands nearby. Quincy nods, gets up, and
follows Frank out of the room, tailed by Cornie.

                    IRENE (CONT'D)
          I NEVER WOULD HAVE GUESSED IT
          THAT I COULD BE SO IN LOVE
          BUT NOW THAT I'VE CONFESSED IT
          I'VE NEVER BEEN SO CERTAIN OF

And then Irene spots George hovering near the kitchen
door, watching her. She nods, almost imperceptibly, at
him and smiles.

He grins back.

                    IRENE (CONT'D)
          YOUR LOVE IS A SEAL UPON MY HEART
          NEVER TO PART
          PLEASE TELL ME THAT IT'S TRUE
          FOREVERMORE IT'S ME AND YOU
          THAT THIS IS FOREVER

At the END OF THE NUMBER, the CROWD APPLAUDS, and Irene
exits stage left.

Dickie hands his baton to the Piano Player, who STRIKES
UP AN EASY TUNE as patrons flood the dance floor. Dickie
follows Irene offstage.


INT. PELICAN - BACK OFFICES

Irene pads softly down the hall, listening carefully.

Dickie runs to catch up to Irene.

                         DICKIE
          Irene! Hold up, will you?

She ignores him, but he drags her to a halt.

                    DICKIE (CONT'D)
          How long is this gonna go on?

A CRASH comes from a nearby office.

                         DICKIE (CONT'D)
              What in --

Irene puts her hand over his mouth.

She goes to the office door and presses her ear to it.
Dickie does the same, standing just behind her.

                         QUINCY (O.S.)
                    That will do, Cornie. Very well,
                    Frank. I will offer you one
                    thousand dollars.

                         FRANK (O.S.)
                    What I know is worth a lot more
                    than that.

A strained beat of silence.

                         QUINCY (O.S.)
                    Why don't you tell me precisely
                    how much you think it is worth,
                    then, and we'll see if I am able
                    to accommodate.

                         FRANK (O.S.)
                    I want ten thousand.

The sounds of a SCUFFLE. A PUNCH.

                         QUINCY (O.S.)
                    Cornie. That will suffice. How
                    much did you say, Frank?

                         FRANK (O.S.)
                    One thousand, Mr. Romano.

                         QUINCY (O.S.)
                    I knew you were a reasonable man.
                    You may go.

FOOTSTEPS COME toward the door.

Irene and Dickie scramble to the side and flatten
themselves against the wall.

The door opens, and FRANK, a waiter, steps halfway into
the hall when:

                         QUINCY (O.S.) (CONT'D)
                    Oh, and Frank. Don't bother
                    returning to work. We don't want
                    our patrons wondering why their
                    waiter has a black eye.

Frank hangs his head, closes the office door, and leaves, his back to Irene and Dickie the whole time.

Irene and Dickie breathe a sigh of relief when he's gone, but Irene immediately goes back to the office door to listen again.

>               QUINCY (O.S.) (CONT'D)
>          He's a loose end I can't afford to
>          leave hanging. Do you understand?

>               CORNIE (O.S.)
>          Yes, Mr. Romano. I'll take care of
>          him.

FOOTSTEPS again.

Irene shoves Dickie down the hallway...


INT. PELICAN - BACKSTAGE

As soon as they reach relative safety behind the curtain backstage, they stop.

But the FOOTSTEPS CONTINUE toward them.

Dickie grabs Irene and kisses her. Hard.

Cornie appears an instant later and sees them.


ON THE OPPOSITE SIDE

George comes around the corner just in time to see it too. Crushed, infuriated, he turns back the way he came.


DICKIE

Waits for Cornie to disappear before he lets Irene come up for air.

Irene draws back and throws a left hook Max Baer would be proud of. It drives Dickie through the curtain and CRASHING into the DRUM SET.

Irene runs.


EXT. PELICAN - BACKSTAGE ENTRANCE

The DOOR BANGS OPEN as Irene runs out.

She looks both ways. Spots Frank just turning the corner
onto the street. She hikes up her dress and pursues.


EXT. STREET

Heads turn and men stare at Irene in her alluring
costume.

Irene doesn't notice. She comes up beside Frank.

                    IRENE
          Frank, isn't it?

                    FRANK
          Miss LeGrange? What are you doing
          out here?

                    IRENE
          I overheard your conversation with
          Quincy.

Frank looks terrified.

                    FRANK
          I don't know what you're talking
          about.

He speeds up his steps, but Irene keeps up.

                    IRENE
          Listen to me, Frank. I have to
          know what you know.

                    FRANK
          Leave me alone. I don't know
          nothin'.

Irene stops and calls out loud enough for other people to
hear.

                    IRENE
          Cornie's got orders to kill you.

Frank halts. Turns. Grabs Irene and ducks into a
sheltered doorway.

                    FRANK
          I ain't gonna talk. You tell him
          I'll be quiet as the grave. Here.

He shoves a thousand dollar bill into her hand.

                    FRANK (CONT'D)
I won't even keep the money. You
give it back to him. I won't tell
a soul.

                    IRENE
What won't you tell a soul?

                    FRANK
What I know. But I don't know
nothin'. You tell Mr. Romano, I
don't know nothin'.

                    IRENE
Is it about Sammy Petruccio's
disappearance?

                    FRANK
Sammy knew too much too. I don't
wanna end up like Sammy. So you
tell him I don't know nothin'. I
was mistaken.

                    IRENE
Did he have Sammy killed?

                    FRANK
Sammy told me he had to get to Mr.
Romano before Cornie did, but he
never said what Cornie had on him.
That's all I know. I don't know
nothin' else.

                    IRENE
He had to get to Quincy. Where?
Where was Sammy going to meet
Quincy?

                    FRANK
I mighta heard him say something
about tuna and ballet. But I don't
know. I told you all I know. I
don't know nothin' else.

                    IRENE
Tuna? That makes no sense.

                    FRANK
I'm tellin' ya. "For tuna and more
ballet." That's what it was. But I
don't know where that is or what
it is or nothin'. I don't know
nothin'.

                    IRENE
          Thank you, Frank. And watch out
          for yourself, huh?

She hands the thousand dollar bill back to him and heads
down the street toward the Pelican.


INT. PELICAN - QUINCY'S OFFICE - SAME

Quincy stares out his window and sips on expensive
scotch.

Cornie enters.

                    QUINCY
          That was quick. Even for you.

                    CORNIE
          Haven't done it yet. Thought you
          might have another job for me when
          you hear what I just seen.

Quincy turns to him, eyebrows raised.

                    CORNIE (CONT'D)
          The bandleader and the canary.
          Lockin' lips.

The only hint of Quincy's fury is a twitch in his jaw. He
says nothing.

                    CORNIE (CONT'D)
          What do you want me to do, boss?

                    QUINCY
          You have two unsavory jobs to do
          tonight, Cornie. The sooner you
          carry them out, the better.

                    CORNIE
          Yes, Mr. Romano.

Cornie leaves.

Quincy stares out the window and calmly, coldly, he sips
his scotch.


INT. SIG'S OFFICE - RECEPTION - DAY

Irene sleeps, head resting on one arm on the desk, the
other hand resting on the phone.

Like she was about to call someone but fell asleep before completing her task. Her glasses are all askew.

Sig comes out of his office.

Irene doesn't wake.

Sig walks up to Irene's desk. He's not amused.

> SIG
> (normal voice)
> Miss Granger.

No response.

> SIG (CONT'D)
> (a little louder)
> Miss Granger.

She twitches slightly, but still doesn't wake.

> SIG (CONT'D)
> (yelling)
> Miss Granger!

Irene sits bolt upright, adjusting her glasses and smoothing back her hair.

> IRENE
> Mr. Pfefferle.

> SIG
> Do you have an illness in the family, Miss Granger? Noisy neighbors? A new boyfriend?

> IRENE
> Sir?

> SIG
> You're clearly not sleeping enough at night if you feel the need to do so during hours for which I pay you to work. You are perilously close to unemployment, Miss Granger.

> IRENE
> Yes, sir. Sorry, sir. It won't happen again.

> SIG
> No. It will not.

He returns to his office.

Irene sighs and puts her chin in her hand.


EXT. PELICAN - FRONT - EVENING

Irene walks past the main doors. Does a double-take when she sees the sign out front.

It now reads "Irene LeGrange and Her Swingin' Band" and sports a black-and-white cutout of her in the dress with the blush-worthy neckline.

                    IRENE
          Oh, no.


INT. PELICAN - STAGE/MAIN ROOM

The Piano Player runs a last minute rehearsal.

                    PIANO PLAYER
          Trumpets, you can back off a
          little there. And 'bones, play out
          a little. All right, let's pick it
          up at measure 104. One... two...
          one-two-three-four.

The BAND PLAYS.

Irene comes running on stage. Looks around. Doesn't find what she's looking for.

Irene approaches the Piano Player.

                    IRENE
          Where's Dickie?

The Piano Player glares at her.

                    PIANO PLAYER
          Funny. I was gonna ask you the
          same question. It's your name out
          front, not mine.

                    IRENE
          But --

The Piano Player waves the BAND TO A STOP.

                         PIANO PLAYER
            All right, that's good, fellas.
            You've got twenty minutes before
            curtain.

The band members disperse.

Irene spots George setting a table.

She runs down the stage stairs and goes over to him.

                         IRENE
            Hey, George, something strange is
            going on here. Have you seen
            Dickie? Or Frank? Or Quincy?

George raises one eyebrow as he glances at her, but he
doesn't reply.

                         IRENE (CONT'D)
            Is that a no?

He ignores her.

                         IRENE (CONT'D)
            George?

                         GEORGE
            I've got work to do.

He pushes past her and disappears into the kitchen.

Irene is hurt. Her bottom lip quivers. But then she
steels herself, gets angry. She will. Not. Cry.

She heads for...


INT. PELICAN - BACK OFFICES

Irene marches up to Quincy's office and knocks on the
door.

                         QUINCY (O.S.)
            Enter.

Irene opens the door and steps inside...


INT. PELICAN - QUINCY'S OFFICE

Quincy looks up from his desk when Irene comes in.

                    QUINCY
         My dear. How unexpected. But
         fortuitous. There's something I
         wanted to speak with you about.


                    IRENE
         Is it about the sign out front?


                    QUINCY
         Do you like it?


                    IRENE
         It's not my band. It's Dickie's.


                    QUINCY
         Yes, Dickie. That's what I wanted
         to discuss with you. Dickie is no
         longer with us.

                    IRENE
         Where is he?

Quincy stands and rounds the desk.

He comes close to Irene. Uncomfortably close. But she
stands her ground.

                    QUINCY
         Dickie tried to take something
         that didn't belong to him.
         Something that belongs to me.

He caresses her cheek with his hand.

                    QUINCY (CONT'D)
         Do you understand, Irene?

His hand slides down to her neck. He rubs his thumb
across her throat.

Tears form in her eyes. Tears of fear. And repulsion.

                    IRENE
         You had him killed? Because of me?

                    QUINCY
         Ugh. "Killed." Such an uncivilized
         word.

He smiles. Leans forward and kisses her on the forehead.

                    QUINCY (CONT'D)
         Good luck, tonight, sweet
         songbird.

He goes to the door and opens it.

Obediently, she leaves.


INT. PELICAN - STAGE - LATER

The Piano Player leads the BAND IN A SLOW BLUES TUNE.

The spotlight hits Irene.

She sings, timid and distracted at first.

                    IRENE
          WE WERE A PERFECT PAIR
          YOU SAID YOU'D ALWAYS CARE
          BUT IT'S BECOMING CLEAR
          I THOUGHT YOU WERE SINCERE
          OUR WHOLE LIVES WE WOULD BE
                SPENDING
          BUT YOU WERE JUST PRETENDING

But as the song goes on, the words -- the music -- pour
out of her with power and rage.

                    IRENE (CONT'D)
          THE NOTES YOU NEVER SENT
          THE PLACE WE NEVER WENT
          THE THOUGHTS YOU'D NEVER SHARE
          I SHOULD HAVE BEEN AWARE
          OF ALL THE HINTS MY HEART WAS
                SENDING
          THAT YOU WERE JUST PRETENDING


AT THE BAR

George glares at Irene as he waits for a drink order.

                    IRENE (CONT'D)
          AT LEAST THE RECORD'S STRAIGHT NOW
          AND FINALLY I SEE
          I BET YOU THINK IT'S GREAT HOW
          THE TRUTH HAS SET YOU FREE

          I SAID I'D BE ALL RIGHT
          'CAUSE NOW I SEE THE LIGHT
          AND I'M NO LONGER BLIND
          I SAID I DIDN'T MIND
          THAT OUR LOVE AFFAIR WAS ENDING
          BUT I WAS JUST PRETENDING

The CROWD GOES CRAZY as she exits stage right.

INT. PELICAN - DRESSING ROOM

Irene opens her door and collapses crying into the chair
in front of the vanity.

When she finally looks up, she sees in the mirror:

Cornie, watching her silently from where he stands
against the wall.

Irene spins in her chair.

                    IRENE
          How long have you been standing
          there?

                    CORNIE
          Does it matter?

                    IRENE
          What do you want? Did Quincy send
          you?

                    CORNIE
          No, Mr. Romano don't know about
          this little visit. This one's just
          between you and me. See, I had
          some very interesting
          conversations with a couple of
          your friends last night.

                    IRENE
          My friends...

                    CORNIE
          Dickie. Frank. Frank seemed a
          little confused, but Dickie was
          very forthcoming about you. What
          you're doing here.

Irene is frozen.

                    CORNIE (CONT'D)
          Quincy's got a real blind spot
          when it comes to beautiful dames,
          but not me. I seen right through
          you from the start.

Cornie steps across the small room and hovers over Irene.
He puts a rough hand under her chin, forcing her to look
up at him.

                    CORNIE (CONT'D)
          So you got two options, doll face.
          Back off trying to find out what
          happened to Sammy, or I spill to
          Quincy. Right?

Irene swats his hand away and stands up. She won't be
bullied.

                    IRENE
          Get out of my dressing room.

For a long, tense beat, it's a stare-down.

Finally, Cornie turns and leaves.

Irene slumps into the chair once again, shaken to her
core.


EXT. PELICAN - BACKSTAGE ENTRANCE - LATER

Irene steps out into the alley. She waits.

The Lead Trumpet and Piano Player come out the door.

She tries to smile at them, but they pay her no
attention.

A sous chef and bartender come out next. They also pass
her by without a word.

She waits.

And waits.


INT. SIG'S OFFICE - RECEPTION - MORNING

Sig paces back and forth, now and then glancing angrily
at Irene's empty desk. He checks his watch.

He waits.

And waits.

Finally, the door opens, and Irene enters. She's a wreck.

                    SIG
          Ah! How considerate of you to come
          to work today.

Irene doesn't seem to register that she's in trouble.

                    IRENE
          Good morning, Mr. Pfefferle.

                    SIG
          Do you even know what time it is?

                    IRENE
          I'm late. I know. I'm sorry, Mr.
          Pfefferle.
                (a beat)
          Can I ask you a question?

Sig raises his eyebrows.

                    IRENE (CONT'D)
          Have you ever been threatened by
          someone you were investigating? Or
          been semi-romantically involved
          with a suspect? Or been
          responsible for a client's...
          death?

                    SIG
          What are you talking about, Miss
          Granger?

Irene takes one of Sig's hands in her own and looks into
his eyes.

                    IRENE
          I owe you an apology, Mr.
          Pfefferle. I never truly
          appreciated how hard your job is.
          The risks involved. It takes great
          strength of character to do what
          you do.

She's not flattering him. She means it.

But it works just as well as flattery. Sig softens. At
least enough not to fire her on the spot.

Sig disengages his hand from hers and shakes his head.

                    SIG
          I'll never understand women.

He disappears into his office.


EXT. PELICAN - FRONT - EVENING

Irene hurries past the doors and the ridiculous sign.

Two beats later, Sig strolls up to the sign. Tilts his head as he studies the cutout...

Irene looks different without her glasses and tasteful ladies' suit, and the name:

                              SIG
                    LeGrange.

Sig goes inside.


INT. PELICAN - FRONT ENTRANCE

Sig hands his overcoat and hat to the hat check girl.

At the host stand:

                              SIG
                    Table for one.

The HOST (50s) grabs a menu and leads Sig into...


INT. PELICAN - MAIN ROOM

The Host leads Sig to a table up front, near the dance floor.

                              SIG
                    No, no. I'd like to sit toward the
                    back. But someplace that has a
                    good view of Miss Irene...

                              HOST
                    LeGrange. Of course. As you wish,
                    sir.

He seats Sig at a table toward the back with a good view of the stage.

                              HOST (CONT'D)
                    Miss LeGrange should be on for her
                    first number shortly, sir.

                              SIG
                    Thank you.

Sig is alone for only a moment before George comes over to take his order.

                              GEORGE
                    Something to drink, sir?

                    SIG
          Whiskey. Neat.

                    GEORGE
          Yes, sir.

George turns to leave, but:

                    SIG
          Waiter. Can you tell me something
          about Miss LeGrange?

George's face darkens.

                    GEORGE
          What do you want to know, sir?

                    SIG
          How long has she worked here?

                    GEORGE
          Not long, sir.

                    SIG
          Do you know where she worked
          before?

                    GEORGE
          No, sir.

                    SIG
          Thank you. You may go.

George nods and leaves.

A beat later the lights dim and a spotlight hits the
stage.

IRENE

steps into the spotlight.

It's a LIGHT-HEARTED NUMBER.

                    IRENE
          AT THE STROKE OF NINE
          I'M FEELING MIGHTY FINE
          I'VE GOT A DATE WITH MACK
          WE'LL BE BALLIN' THE JACK

Irene makes her way around the dance floor, teasing
patrons at the surrounding tables.

                              IRENE (CONT'D)
                    AT THE STROKE OF TEN
                    READY TO GO AGAIN
                    MEET ME ON THE ROOFTOP
                    WE'LL BE DOIN' THE HOP


SIG

Betrays little emotion as he watches her.

                              IRENE
                    AT THE STROKE OF ELEVEN
                    I'M IN DANCING HEAVEN
                    I DON'T MEAN TO BRAG
                    WE'LL BE DOIN' THE SHAG


GEORGE

Puts in an order at the bar in a voice inappropriately
loud during a performance.

                         GEORGE
                    One whiskey. Neat.

The patrons seated at the bar all "shush" him.


IRENE

Looks in the direction of the commotion.

George's back is to her.

                              IRENE
                    MIDNIGHT COMES AND GOES
                    I COULD JITTERBUG ALL NIGHT
                    I'LL KEEP YOU ON YOUR TOES
                    UNTIL THE MORNING LIGHT


THE BARTENDER

Glares at George and shakes his head before turning to
pour the whiskey.


QUINCY AND CORNIE

Watch from a spot on the upper level.

Quincy can't take his eyes off of Irene, but Cornie's
eyes constantly flick to Quincy.

                              IRENE
              AT THE STROKE OF ONE
              I'M NOT EVEN CLOSE TO DONE
              I'LL FIND MY DANCING KING
              AND WE'LL SWING, SWING, SWING


SIG

Takes in the CROWD'S REACTION when the SONG ENDS.

They love Irene.


INT. PELICAN - DRESSING ROOM - LATER

Behind the dressing screen, Irene is halfway out of her
dress when there's a KNOCK.

                              IRENE
                    Just a moment.

But the door opens, and Sig comes in.

Irene couldn't be more shocked.

                              IRENE (CONT'D)
                    Mr. Pfefferle!

She hurriedly drags her dressing gown from where it hangs
over the screen and slips it on. She comes from behind
the screen.

                              IRENE (CONT'D)
                    I can explain --

Sig holds up a hand to stop her. Then turns it palm up.

                              SIG
                    Your key, Miss Granger.

                              IRENE
                    My what?

                              SIG
                    Your key. To my office. You won't
                    be needing it anymore.

It takes a moment for the words to sink in.

Finally, Irene nods and goes to her clutch on the vanity.
She pulls out the office key and hands it to Sig.

Without another word, he leaves.

EXT. PELICAN - BACKSTAGE ENTRANCE - LATER

Irene waits.

The sous chef and bartender come out the door.

Then the Bari Sax.

Then George.

Irene ambushes him.

> IRENE
> What's with you, George Carpenter?
> Ignoring me? Interrupting my
> performance? Don't think I didn't
> notice.

> GEORGE
> Oh, I'm sorry. Do you think your
> vanity will recover after such a
> grievous injury?

> IRENE
> Vanity? You think I'm vain?

> GEORGE
> Is there another reason a woman
> strings...
>         (does a mental count)
> Five different men along?

> IRENE
> What are you talking about?

George counts them off on his fingers for her.

> GEORGE
> Dickie. Romano. Frank. Some square
> I served tonight. I don't know,
> maybe Cornie's in on the action
> too. I guess that makes six when
> you count the prize fool of them
> all: George Henry Carpenter.

Irene is overwhelmed at the list of names. Doesn't even
know where to begin.

George starts to walk away.

> IRENE
> Wait --

Irene grabs his SLEEVE to stop him, and it RIPS at the
shoulder.

                    IRENE (CONT'D)
          Oh --

Now George is really steamed. Irene releases his sleeve,
and he walks away again.

Irene runs around in front of him to block his progress.

                    IRENE (CONT'D)
          George. George, I can explain
          everything. All of it. It's not
          what you think. I'm not who you
          think I am.

                    GEORGE
          Save it. I saw you and Dickie with
          my own eyes.

It takes a moment for Irene to figure out what George
means, and he steps around her and walks away again. But
then she remembers:

                    IRENE
          You saw him kiss me. Backstage.

George keeps walking, but Irene runs around in front of
him again. He tries to sidestep, but she plays good
defense.

                    IRENE (CONT'D)
          Look --

He jukes one way and tries to go the other, but he can't
fool her -- she backs him into the wall.

                    IRENE (CONT'D)
          Look, I'm sorry about that. But if
          you'd hung around, you would've
          also seen me sock Dickie right in
          the kisser... if you'll excuse the
          expression.

George is a little bit impressed. But he's also stubborn.

                    GEORGE
          He wouldn't kiss you if he didn't
          think you wanted to be kissed. I
          know Dickie.

Irene is torn between frustration and grief.

                    IRENE
          You __knew__ Dickie. It doesn't matter
          if I wanted him to or not, or if
          he even thought I wanted him to.
          All that really matters is he's
          dead because he kissed me.

This is news to George. She's got his attention now.

IN THE BACKGROUND, Quincy's town car rolls to a stop at
the intersection of the alley and the street.

Neither Irene nor George notices.

Irene gathers her courage. Takes a breath. Dives in.

                    IRENE (CONT'D)
          My name isn't Irene LeGrange. It's
          Irene Granger.

                    GEORGE
          You have a stage name. That's not
          unusual.

                    IRENE
          Will you shut up and listen? What
          I'm telling you is I'm not even a
          singer. At least I wasn't until I
          came to the Pelican. I'm a
          secretary. For a private
          investigator. Or was until I got
          fired tonight. That square you
          served... ten to one that was my
          boss, Sig Pfefferle. He must've
          followed me here. He didn't know I
          was...
                    (backs up in the
                     story)
          Dickie hired Sig to find out what
          happened to Sammy Petruccio. But
          Sig didn't find anything. He told
          Dickie it was a dead end. Only I
          knew there had to be a connection
          to Quincy. So I started my own
          investigation...


INT. TOWN CAR - SAME

Unbeknownst to Irene and George, Quincy and Cornie watch
them through the window, but can't hear their
conversation.

Irene uses her hands when she talks. She's very excited.

Quincy's eyes narrow and his jaw twitches.

                    QUINCY
          What's his name?

                    CORNIE
          George Carpenter. He's a waiter.
          What do you want me to do about
          him?

                    QUINCY
          Nothing. Yet. Unless you possess
          some savvy about the nature of
          their relationship that I do not.

Cornie doesn't reply.

Quincy turns to him.

                    QUINCY (CONT'D)
          Do you?

Cornie shakes his head.

Quincy turns back to the window.


EXT. PELICAN - BACKSTAGE ENTRANCE - SAME

Irene comes to the end of her story.

George looks like he's following... mostly.

                    IRENE
          I don't know what Cornie did to
          make him talk, but Dickie gave me
          up. And it's only a matter of time
          before Cornie tells Quincy.

George takes a moment to process all he's heard.

                    GEORGE
          You and me. Was that real? Or were
          you only using me to dig up
          information about Sammy?

Irene takes a step closer. Smiles slightly.

                    IRENE
          How could I use you when you
          didn't even know enough to be
          useful?

George pulls her another step closer.

                         GEORGE
               Then tell me this. Am I in love
               with Irene LeGrange? Or Irene
               Granger?

She grabs his lapels.

                         IRENE
               I don't know. But I know they're
               both in love with you.

She kisses him.

IN THE BACKGROUND, Quincy's town car pulls forward until
it's out of sight.

Suddenly, Irene breaks the kiss.

                         IRENE (CONT'D)
               George, wait. What happened to
               Dickie... I couldn't bear it --

George stops her words with his own kiss.


INT. TOWN CAR - SAME

Quincy gazes out the window, his calm more frightening
than any fit of rage would be.

                         CORNIE
               Broad ain't too bright, is she? So
               do I bump him off?

                         QUINCY
               I hate when you say it that way.
               It's ugly.

A beat.

Cornie waits.

                         QUINCY (CONT'D)
               Anyway, I have a better idea.
                    (to the driver)
               Stop the car.

The car pulls over.

                         QUINCY (CONT'D)
                    (to Cornie)
               Telephone my cousin. Have him meet
               me at La Fortuna in an hour.

Cornie gets out of the car.

                         QUINCY (CONT'D)
                    (to the driver)
               Back to the Pelican.


EXT. STREET - SAME

Irene and George walk side-by-side down the sidewalk.

Quincy's town car turns onto the street at the
intersection in front of them.

Irene recognizes it immediately and turns toward a
darkened shop window, pretending to study the mannequin
inside.

George stops, confused.

Irene doesn't look away from the shop window.

                         IRENE
               Quincy. Keep walking.

George does as he's told.

Quincy's car crosses lanes and pulls up to the curb next
to Irene. The back door opens and Quincy steps out.

He holds the door for Irene.

                         QUINCY
               My darling songbird. Please.

Irene swallows nervously and gets in.

Further up the sidewalk, almost at the street corner,
George risks a worried glance back at her.

Quincy follows Irene inside.

The car pulls away.

                         GEORGE
               I hope you know what you're doing.


INT. TOWN CAR - SAME

Quincy locks eyes with Irene. She doesn't flinch.

Finally, he smiles.

                         QUINCY
          I have a surprise for you, my
          dear.

He reaches into a coat pocket.

Irene holds her breath.

But when his hand comes out, he's holding a small velvet
box. A ring box. He pops open the lid. Inside is the
biggest rock Irene has ever seen.

Her eyes widen.

                         QUINCY (CONT'D)
          Do you like it?

                         IRENE
          It's lovely.

                         QUINCY
          Dear, sweet songbird. I realize
          how much I must have upset you the
          other night. After all, I made my
          expectations of you clear. But it
          must seem terribly unfair -- no,
          it is terribly unfair -- to make
          such demands without offering
          anything in return.

                         IRENE
          What are you offering?

Quincy laughs.

                         QUINCY
          Marriage, of course. It's rather a
          clumsy proposal, I'm afraid. But a
          sincere one, nonetheless.

                         IRENE
          Quincy, I...

She starts to shake her head.

Quincy SNAPS the BOX SHUT.

                         QUINCY
          I should advise you to consider
          your answer very carefully, my
          dear. The waiter -- George? --
          yes, George's life is wholly
          dependent upon it.

Irene does her best to betray no emotion.

> IRENE
> Marriage is a serious step for a
> girl like me. I need time to think
> about it.

Quincy smirks.

> QUINCY
> Time to think about it? Or time to
> warn George?

Angry tears well up in her eyes.

> IRENE
> Why would you want to marry
> someone you know doesn't love you?

Quincy opens the box again, takes out the ring, and slips
it on Irene's finger.

> QUINCY
> You'll learn. In time.

The tears spill over and slide down her cheeks.


EXT. IRENE'S APARTMENT BUILDING - LATER

Quincy's town car rolls to a stop in front of those same
steps where Irene and George danced into each other's
hearts.

The door opens and Irene steps out.

From inside the car:

> QUINCY
> Sweet dreams, sweet songbird.

Irene doesn't even look back at him. She walks up the
steps and into the building.

Once she disappears from view, the car rolls away.

One beat.

Two beats.

Three beats.

Irene pokes her head out the door. Seeing that the car is
gone, she races back down the steps.

INT. GEORGE'S APARTMENT - LATER

George paces restlessly. FRANTIC KNOCKING at the DOOR
brings him to a halt.

                    IRENE (O.S.)
          George, it's me. George.

George crosses to the door and opens it.

Irene flies into his arms.

          GEORGE                        IRENE (CONT'D)
Thank goodness, you're all      You're all right, thank
right.                          goodness.

Irene pushes away just enough to look into George's eyes.

                    IRENE (CONT'D)
          Let's leave the city. Go live on a
          farm or a ranch. Or some tropical
          island. Let's leave tonight. Right
          now. Never look back.

                    GEORGE
          What happened with Romano?

She holds up her left hand. Shows him the ring.

George whistles appreciatively.

                    IRENE
          He knows about us. About you. He
          said if I don't marry him...

She can't even finish the disgusting thought.

                    IRENE (CONT'D)
          Please, George. Let's just leave.
          Go somewhere he can't find us.

George kisses the tip of her nose.

                    GEORGE
          No, my love. If we want to be
          really and truly free, we have to
          see this thing through. Finish
          what you started. Find the
          evidence that ties Romano to
          Sammy's disappearance and Dickie's
          death. Put him and his goons away
          for good.

Irene nods, courage returning.

                         IRENE
              Okay.


INT. GEORGE'S APARTMENT - LATER

George sits at a table writing notes as Irene paces the
room, spilling everything she knows, everything she's
gathered so far.

                         IRENE
              I figure Sammy must have been one
              of Quincy's lackeys. Family
              business, right? I did some
              digging in their vital records.
              They were second cousins once
              removed, or first cousins twice
              removed, or something. Anyway, I
              know for a fact Sammy was on
              Quincy's yacht. A lot.

                         GEORGE
              How do you know?

                         IRENE
              I found this.

Irene pulls the cigarette case engraved with "S.P." from
her clutch and sets in on the table in front of George.

George picks it up and frowns as he inspects it.

                         IRENE (CONT'D)
              And lots of appointments in
              Quincy's date book with the same
              initials. S-P. Sammy Petruccio.

                         GEORGE
              But Sammy didn't smoke.

Irene stops her pacing.

George smiles a bit.

                         GEORGE (CONT'D)
              Maybe you can use me after all.

                         IRENE
              But the initials --

                         GEORGE
              Sammy had asthma. Said cigarette
              smoke made it too hard for him
              play his trombone.

Irene is stumped.

                    GEORGE (CONT'D)
          You know what gets me?

                    IRENE
          Hmm.

                    GEORGE
          Why Cornie bothered to threaten
          you. If he knew who you were, what
          you were up to, why didn't he just
          go straight to Quincy?

Irene ponders this question for a beat or two. As the
pieces come together in her mind, her speech gets faster
and faster:

                    IRENE
          Frank said Sammy knew too much and
          was trying to get to Quincy before
          Cornie did. I thought it was
          because Cornie had something on
          Sammy, but what if it was the
          other way around? What if Sammy
          knew something about Cornie?
          Something Cornie didn't want
          Quincy to know. Maybe Cornie was
          afraid I'd find out whatever he's
          trying to hide from Quincy.

                    GEORGE
          I'm not sure I followed all that,
          but it sounded great.

Irene rolls her eyes and takes a seat.

                    IRENE
          Don't you see? Cornie's hiding
          something from Quincy. He's not
          worried that my investigation will
          expose Quincy. He's worried I'm
          going to expose him.

George takes a beat to process.

                    GEORGE
          Then maybe Quincy didn't have
          anything to do with Sammy's
          disappearance at all. Maybe Cornie
          did it on his own.

Irene falls into deep thought again.

                    IRENE
             (slowly; annunciating
              each word)
        "For tuna and more ballet."
             (normal speed)
        Does that mean anything to you?


                    GEORGE
        That you haven't slept in weeks?


                    IRENE
        No, it's where Frank said Sammy
        was going to meet Quincy the night
        he disappeared.
             (slowly)
        "For tuna and more ballet."


                    GEORGE
             (normal speed)
        "For tuna" what?


                    IRENE
        Fortuna! That's it! Quincy's
        yacht: La Fortuna è Mobile. The
        answer must be there. That's where
        we have to look.


                    GEORGE
        What about Quincy?


                    IRENE
        I can keep him occupied long
        enough for you to poke around,
        look for clues.


                    GEORGE
        Occupied?


Irene gives him an apologetic look.

George considers.

                    GEORGE (CONT'D)
        Well... I don't like it. But it'll
        have to do.


EXT. MARINA - JUST BEFORE DAWN

Irene approaches La Fortuna alone.

Cornie stands guarding the gangway.

                    IRENE
          I need to see Quincy.

                    CORNIE
          Mr. Romano is busy.

                    IRENE
          Maybe you don't know, Mr. Mulloy,
          but I'm Quincy's fiancée now. I
          believe that gives me certain
          freedoms... such as boarding La
          Fortuna at my discretion.

She tries to walk past him, but he blocks her way.

                    CORNIE
          What do you want to see him about?

Irene playfully pats him on the cheek.

                    IRENE
          I'll tell you when you're older.

He grabs her wrist, and she gasps in pain.

                    CORNIE
          I said, he's busy.

Irene returns his scowl, in pain but unafraid.

                    IRENE
          Then I'll wait in the guest suite.
          He did say it was mine to use
          whenever I please.

                    CORNIE
          You think you can fool Mr. Romano?
          You think he don't know what a
          tramp you are?

                    IRENE
          What's the matter, Cornie?
          Jealous?

Furious, Cornie turns and drags her up the gangway.

Two beats after they disappear around the corner, George
slips silently up the gangway and heads in the opposite
direction.

INT. YACHT - PASSAGEWAY

Cornie drags Irene roughly along the corridor toward the guest suite.

As they pass the door to Quincy's study, Irene purposely trips and TUMBLES NOISILY to the ground.

> CORNIE
> Get up.

> IRENE
> (loudly)
> You don't have to be so rough --

The door to Quincy's study opens.

Quincy steps out quickly, shutting the door behind him before Irene can identify the other man inside.

Quincy is horrified to see Irene on the ground, her wrist still clenched in Cornie's fist.

A beat too late, Cornie releases her.

Quincy bends to help Irene to her feet.

> QUINCY
> What is the meaning of this, Cornie? My dear, are you hurt?

> IRENE
> If I'm going to be your wife, Quincy, you're going to have to teach this brute some manners.

> QUINCY
> Indeed. Come, my dear.
> (to Cornie)
> Return to your post. Immediately.

Quincy puts an arm around Irene, who leans on him and feigns a limp as they make their way down the hall.

Cornie disappears in the other direction, fuming.

> QUINCY (CONT'D)
> I'm terribly sorry, darling, but as soon as I deposit you in the lounge, I must return to my study. I am just in the middle of a very important business meeting.

                          IRENE
              Of course. But...

                          QUINCY
              Yes?

Irene spares no charm, uses her most sultry voice:

                          IRENE
              Must we go all the way to the
              lounge? Wouldn't the guest <u>bedroom</u>
              be closer?


INT. YACHT - CREW'S QUARTERS - SAME

George peeks around a corner.

Sneaks down the corridor.

Pokes his head in one door and, not finding what he
wants, shuts it again.

Another door. Another bust.

He hears VOICES at the other end of the corridor.

He slips inside the nearest room.


INT. YACHT - CORNIE'S ROOM

George latches the door silently. Turns around and
surveys the tiny room.

On the bed stand is a framed photograph: a family
portrait of Cornie, scowling as always, and a sweet-
looking old woman. It's an odd juxtaposition.

George picks it up curiously.

                          GEORGE
              Bingo.

He puts the photograph down and begins rummaging around
in drawers and under the mattress.

He pulls out a stack of letters from one corner of the
mattress.

                          GEORGE (CONT'D)
              What have we here?

CLOSE ON

A gun sticks into George's back.


GEORGE

Raises his hands in the air, dropping the stack of
letters.


INT. YACHT - GUEST SUITE - SAME

Quincy lowers Irene onto a divan.

                    IRENE
          Thank you.
                (an afterthought)
          Darling.

Quincy looks down at her. He's not buying the new act.

                    QUINCY
          I wonder... What could possibly
          explain this drastic alteration of
          attitude over the course of only a
          few short hours?

                    IRENE
          If I seemed ungracious before, it
          was only because you took me by
          surprise. This has all happened so
          quickly. After all, Quincy, we
          hardly know each other.

                    QUINCY
          Let's don't pretend. I think we
          know one another quite well
          enough, Miss LeGrange. Or shall I
          say, Miss Granger?

Irene's eyes widen.

Before she can respond, George appears in the open
doorway, hands raised.

As George enters, the one who has him at gunpoint is
REVEALED: Sig Pfefferle.

Irene springs to her feet in surprise, fake injury
forgotten.

Quincy watches her reaction with relish.

> QUINCY (CONT'D)
> Miss Granger, I believe you know
> my cousin, Sig Pfefferle. Cousin
> by marriage, of course, but family
> is family.

Sig pokes George in the back, urging him forward.

> SIG
> Go on. Over by Miss Granger.
>         (to Quincy)
> I caught this jerk snooping around
> Cornie's room. But I think you
> oughta see what he found.

> QUINCY
> Very well. I leave these two in
> your capable hands.

Quincy exits the room.

Sig keeps his gun trained on George and Irene, standing
next to each other now.

> SIG
> Take a seat. Make yourselves
> comfortable.

George and Irene sink onto the divan.

Sig sits in a chair next to the door, careful to keep his
aim on his prisoners.

> GEORGE
>         (whispers)
> I thought you said the square was
> a private investigator.

> IRENE
>         (whispers)
> He was. Is. Think about it. It's
> the perfect cover to keep the cops
> off Quincy's back. Brilliant,
> actually. And all this time, I
> thought he was such a lame-brain.

> SIG
> Either speak up so the whole class
> can hear, or zip it.

> IRENE
> I was only complimenting you, Mr.
> Pfefferle.
>         (MORE)

                         IRENE (CONT'D)
              All this time, I thought you had
              absolutely zero talent, but it
              turns out, you are quite adept at
              lying.

                         SIG
              And you, Miss Granger, have always
              proven quite adept at getting on
              my nerves. Which in this
              situation...
                    (waves his gun)
              I wouldn't recommend.

Irene crosses her arms, more annoyed than anything.

                         IRENE
                    (whispers to George)
              What did you find in Cornie's
              room, anyhow?

                         SIG
              Hey!

Irene glares at him.

                         IRENE
                    (much too loudly)
              I said, "what did you find in
              Cornie's room, anyhow?"

                         GEORGE
              A stack of letters from Peaches
              O'Reilly.

                         IRENE
              The Irish mob boss?

                         GEORGE
              Aye.

Putting the pieces together:

                         IRENE
              Cornie was a mole. Trying to
              undermine Quincy's operation, no
              doubt. That's what Sammy must've
              stumbled onto.

                         SIG
              What's that?

                         IRENE
              Sammy Petruccio.

                         SIG
          Yes, I know who Sammy was. I knew
          him quite well, in fact, seeing as
          how he was my mother-in-law's
          second cousin twice removed.

                         IRENE
          Well, whatever reason Cornie gave
          Quincy to have Sammy knocked off
          was bogus. Cornie wanted Sammy
          dead because Sammy knew what he --
          Cornie -- was really up to.

A beat as George and Sig process her logic.

                         SIG
          How did you --

GUNSHOTS RING OUT from somewhere.

They all stand in surprise.

Sig looks out the door.

                         SIG (CONT'D)
          So long, Cornie.

With Sig distracted, Irene's hand flies to her hair. She
whips out a hatpin -- thicker, stronger than before, but
just as sharp -- and flicks her wrist to throw it.

It sticks!

... in the doorway next to Sig's head.

But his surprise provides enough of an opening for George
to bowl into him and tackle him to the ground.

George grapples with Sig for the gun.

They roll over one another until Sig has George pinned.

George throws a punch, knocking Sig backwards and the gun
flying free.

Irene starts toward the gun, but...

QUINCY

Appears in the doorway, his own gun drawn.

IRENE

Puts a hand to her chest and flings her sunburst-shaped brooch like a throwing star.

It hits Quincy in his shooting hand, embedding itself deep into the flesh.

He drops the gun.

Irene dives forward to grab it, ducking under Quincy's flying fist.

Her foot kicks the pistol, sending it spinning across the floor.

Quincy grabs Irene around the waist and pulls her backwards.

GEORGE

Knocks Sig out with another fist to the face.

He grabs Sig's pistol and gets to his feet. He aims the gun at Quincy.

                    GEORGE
          Hold it, Mr. Romano.

Quincy releases Irene.

Irene rushes forward to pick up the discarded gun.

                    GEORGE (CONT'D)
          I've got him, Irene. Call the
          police.

Irene goes to the bed stand and picks up the telephone.

                    IRENE
          Ship to shore.
              (a beat)
          I need the police and an ambulance
          sent to the marina right away.
          Quincy Romano's yacht. La Fortuna
          è Mobile.

                    QUINCY
          Quite fickle indeed.

INT. SIG'S OFFICE - DAY

Irene oversees several movers gutting the office of furniture.

Marjorie, chewing on a rope of licorice, is there for moral support.

>                    MARJORIE
>           I still don't understand why you
>           don't keep it all. Go into
>           business for yourself.

>                    IRENE
>           After this?

Irene grabs a newspaper from her desk just as two burly men start hauling it away. She hands it to Marjorie.

Irene's face is plastered on the front page next to a picture of Quincy being arrested and a publicity shot of Dickie.

The headline reads: "BANDLEADER DICKIE HUGGINS MURDERED." A sub-head reads: "CRIME-SOLVING CANARY CRACKS CASE; QUINCY ROMANO ARRESTED."

>                    MARJORIE
>           Looks like good publicity to me.

>                    IRENE
>           If it weren't for me, Dickie would
>           still be alive. Solving a murder I
>           caused hardly qualifies as good
>           investigative work.

>                    MARJORIE
>           But you also solved Sammy's
>           murder. And unmasked Pfefferle as
>           a dirty fraud. You brought down a
>           crime boss the cops have been
>           trying to nab for years. That's
>           got to count for something.

>                    IRENE
>           Sure. But look at this.
>                (slaps the newspaper)
>           Now the whole city knows my face,
>           how could I ever go undercover
>           again?

                    MARJORIE
          Who says you'd have to? Just be
          yourself. Irene Granger, Private
          Investigator.

Irene considers. She likes the sound of that. But:

                    IRENE
          Who am I kidding? I can't afford a
          space like this.

                    MARJORIE
          Sure you can.

Marjorie points to the huge diamond still perched on
Irene's left ring finger.

                    IRENE
          I couldn't.

                    MARJORIE
          Why not? It's yours. He gave it to
          you.

                    IRENE
          Under false pretenses. I should
          give it back.

Irene holds up her hand, mesmerized by the sparkling
stone.

                    MARJORIE
          Irene. He's a murderer. I think
          God will forgive you if you sell
          his ring so you can catch more
          murderers.
               (a beat)
          Besides, how do you think George
          feels about you still having that
          thing on your finger?

Irene takes it off immediately and stuffs it into her
clutch.


EXT. PELICAN - DAY

Not only is the ridiculous sign advertising Irene
LeGrange and Her Band gone... Men on ladders work to take
down the bright neon "Pelican" sign above the doors.

George watches their progress from a bench on the
opposite side of the street.

Irene takes a seat next to him.

                    IRENE
        Is this what you wanted me to see?
        In case I forgot that, because of
        me, we're both out of a job now?

The men on the ladders lower the "Pelican" sign to men standing below.

George smiles.

                    GEORGE
        Speak for yourself. I happen to be
        gainfully employed at this
        establishment.

                    IRENE
        What establishment?

George nods toward the new sign going up over the doors:

"Cafe LeGrange"

Irene's mouth falls open.

                    GEORGE
        I had trouble deciding between
        "Chez LeGrange" and "Cafe
        LeGrange." Neither really makes
        sense in French, not to mention
        it's completely incorrect
        grammatically, but... I kinda like
        it. What do you think?

                    IRENE
        <u>You</u> had trouble deciding?

                    GEORGE
        Sure. I told you I wanted to run
        the joint someday.

                    IRENE
        But how --

                    GEORGE
        And I thought I might ask this
        crime-solving singer I know to
        headline the show. She's dynamite.
        But I'm worried she might turn me
        down.

                    IRENE
          But where did you get the money to
          buy -- crime-solving singer? You
          mean me?


                    GEORGE
          I was also thinking of proposing
          to her, but...

                    IRENE
          But what?

                    GEORGE
          We haven't known each other that
          long --

                    IRENE
          Yes.

                    GEORGE
          And I haven't been completely
          honest with her --

                    IRENE
          I said yes -- wait, what? Honest
          about what?

                    GEORGE
          See, she thinks I'm a charming,
          but penniless waiter. But the
          truth is...

                    IRENE
          Yes?


                    GEORGE
          I'm a boring, but wealthy
          investor. I own some shares in
          this company that's using a new
          synthetic material called nylon to
          make toothbrushes. They're selling
          like hotcakes.


                    IRENE
          Toothbrushes?

                    GEORGE
          Do you mind?

Bewildered, confused, speechless, Irene can only look
back and forth between George and the new Cafe LeGrange.

INT. CAFE LEGRANGE - MAIN ROOM - NIGHT

The joint is jumpin'.

George, looking sharp in his dinner jacket, greets finely
dressed patrons as they enter.

Two of those patrons are Marjorie and a timid, geeky-
looking guy that she clings to giddily.

She shows off her brand new engagement ring to George,
and her beau blushes all the way to the tips of his ears.

George personally escorts them to a VIP table.


THE PIANO PLAYER

Leads the BAND on stage in a SWING TUNE, and folks crowd
the dance floor.


GEORGE

Checks his watch and excuses himself.


INT. CAFE LEGRANGE - DRESSING ROOM - SAME

Irene stands in front of the full-length mirror.

From a small table next to her, she grabs a hatpin --
thick, strong, sharp -- and slides it through her updo.

Next, she attaches a sparkling, sunburst-shaped brooch to
the front of her elegant, but modest gown.

A simple wedding band graces her left ring finger.

Last of all, she puts Quincy's ring on her right hand.
Makes a fist and punches it into her other palm.

Satisfied with the effect, she breathes on the diamond
and shines it.

She twirls in the mirror. Smiles at her reflection.


INT. CAFE LEGRANGE - STAGE

It starts with the DRUMS beating out a MARCHING RHYTHM.

As the BRASS PLAYS A FANFARE, dancers -- men and women --
pour out from both sides of the stage and down the stairs
to the dance floor.

The rest of the BAND JOINS IN, and the dancers
synchronize in Busby Berkeley-style choreography.

Irene and George meet in the middle of the stage.

>                    GEORGE
>           I FEEL LIKE CLAPPIN' AND TAPPIN'
>           DRUMMIN' AND SNAPPIN'
>           MY HEART IS THUMPIN' AND JUMPIN'
>                FOR JOY
>           MY HEART IS HAPPY, HAPPY TO SAY
>                I'M YOUR BOY


>                    IRENE
>           I FEEL LIKE CROONIN' AND SWOONIN'
>           HUGGIN' AND SPOONIN'
>           MY HEART IS SINGIN' AND SPRINGIN'
>                TO LIFE
>           MY HEART IS HAPPY, HAPPY TO SAY
>                I'M YOUR WIFE

They dance. The other dancers swirl around them. Separate
them. Weave in and out between them. Bring them back
together.

>                    CHORUS
>           THE SKIES ARE CLEARING
>           THE CLOUDS ARE DISAPPEARING
>           THE FUTURE'S BRIGHT NOW
>           EVERYTHING'S ALL RIGHT NOW


>                 GEORGE AND IRENE
>           I FEEL LIKE PLAYIN' AND SWAYIN'
>           WITH YOU ALWAYS STAYIN'
>           MY HEART IS REELIN' AND FEELIN' SO
>                FINE
>           MY HEART IS HAPPY, HAPPY TO SAY
>                THAT YOU'RE MINE

As the MUSIC BUILDS TO A CLIMAX, Irene twirls into
George's arms. They kiss.

>                                        FADE OUT.


                              THE END

## WRITER'S NOTE

Old movie musicals are the best, and I would give almost anything to see that genre revived on the big screen. Movies like *La La Land* and *The Greatest Showman* have been some solace, but too few and far between. Until that glorious age of musicals returns, publishing this screenplay as a book will suffice. I'm just happy that, like "Bergman Manor," this story is now out in the world for people to enjoy instead of collecting cyber-dust in my computer files.

This is the first feature script I ever wrote just for myself. It wasn't an assignment or a collaboration or a request from anyone else. It's purely my own, even the lyrics. (These songs represent my very first attempt at writing lyrics, by the way, so don't judge me too harshly.)

The idea came to me when I was going through a Sam Spade/Philip Marlowe kind of phase in my movie watching. In all these hardboiled detective movies, the detective relies on his secretary's help and confidence and instincts -- but most of these movies never really develop the secretary into a three-dimensional character. She's more like a really useful prop.

Well, I thought it would be interesting to make her a real character and tell *her* story for a change. From there, the ideas just kept coming. What if she were a better detective than her boss? What if she went undercover as a singer? Then I could make it a musical because I love musicals! The case of the missing trombone player! YES! It started to write itself after that.

This script was such a joy for me to write, and I sincerely hope that it has been a joy for you to read.

Many blessings to you and yours!

## ACKNOWLEDGMENTS

I have to start by acknowledging the two people for whom the main characters are named: my grandparents, George and Irene Bell. Growing up, I heard many stories about how much Grandpa George and Grandma Irene loved to dance in their younger days -- and that they were darn good at it, too! Grandpa George and Grandma Irene, I miss you both dearly, and I pray that you are dancing together in heaven!

I also need to give a shout out to my cover designer, Bilal Abiyhasa. This is our second project together, and I can't offer enough praise for his work. I know my covers are in good hands with you, Abi!

Many thanks to all the family members, friends, and colleagues who have read my scripts, given me notes, and cheered me on over the years. Your generosity and love humble me.

Above all, I must give all thanks and praise to Christ, my Divine Spouse. I am nothing without Him: "Whom have I in heaven but Thee? And there is nothing upon earth that I desire besides Thee. My flesh and my heart may fail, but God is the strength of my heart and my portion for ever" (Ps 73:25-26).

## ABOUT THE WRITER

Tara started writing fiction when she was in first grade, but she didn't discover the thrill of screenwriting until she studied Communications Media at John Paul the Great Catholic University. Screenplays are her favorite way to tell stories.

Tara resides in Colorado, and in 2016, she became a Consecrated Virgin Living in the World in the Diocese of Colorado Springs. In addition to making things up and writing them down, Tara enjoys praying, hiking (definitely not running), going to the symphony (especially movies at the symphony), discovering new craft brews, and spending time with family and friends.

CPSIA information can be obtained
at www.ICGtesting.com
Printed in the USA
LVHW060030160620
658145LV00011B/764

9 781734 914221